D1602503

LOVE AND THE MESS WE'RE IN

ALSO BY STEPHEN MARCHE

Raymond + Hannah
Shining At The Bottom Of The Sea
Lucy Hardin's Missing Period
How Shakespeare Changed Everything

Love and the Mess We're In Love and the Mess We

ove and the Mess We're In Love and the Mess We're In Love and the Mess We're In Lo

Stephen Marche

d the Mess We're In Love and the Mess We're In Love

Love and the
Mess We're In

GASPEREAU PRESS LIMITED · PRINTERS & PUBLISHERS · MMXII

To Sarah

1

A Night in Buenos Aires

Separately, suddenly, Clive and Viv remember the smell of pine trees. He's in the waiting area at the arrivals gate, shifting on a segmented bench nobody ever sat on happily, and she's straightening to exit the plane in an orderly fashion, her neck bent by the window seat curve. Between them all the restlessness of the Buenos Aires airport, the usual decrepit haunted house of commerce and exile and tourism, its hallways sleek with strangers' shoulders hunched under baggage, desperate with anxious exhausted eyes upturning to clocks and sliding doors, livid with bored blandness. But there is the smell of pines. The smell of the strength of life in all seasons.

The sliding door glides open

Clive? All these strangers rubbing together
like a hundred curtains behind a hundred
draughty windows and there's Clive there
he is there he is

In the crush of distance-clinchers, like
angel-wrestlers, like slo-mo sumos and
we'll be like that me and there she is

The sliding door glides closed

Viv
I've got a line.

Clive
Do tell.

Viv
I don't know how I'm ever going to forgive myself for what I'm about to do with you. That's
my line. I've been thinking about it ever since I
got on the plane last night.

Clive
I've been not thinking.

No need to wait (Viv trundling just carry-on)
and the awkwardness of their bodies (whose
bodies?) separating from the embrace, the dis-
comfort (not husband, not boyfriend) of their
strides turning (to hold hands?) out of place
(who is with whom?) to the taxi (who pays?)
adulterers' stutter-steps.

ADULTERY

Viv's husband Tim is Clive's best friend, and Tim now lives in an institution for the insane in the small town of Newmarket.

Neither Clive nor Viv would recognize themselves in their own story, because they are not the kind of people who do what they're about to do. If you told Clive about a man going to cheat with his oldest friend's wife, he would frown and ask "Who could do that?" Viv, the dedicated wife who suspended her writing career to care for her ill husband, was willing to endure an entire day of air travel, with a ten-hour delay in Atlanta, to walk out of the Aeropuerta Internacional Ministro Pistarini De Ezeiza, into a rainy evening with another man.

The thing about adultery is that we say, "you commit it." You commit adultery. Who came up with that? I mean you commit adultery because you cannot commit. That's the whole point. You thought you could but you can't. And then the word "adultery." What's adult about it? It should be called adolescentery. "Yeah, I caught her committing adolescentery. And with my best friend." Much better. Either that or "He couldn't commit adultery. So he ran off with his secretary, the bastard."

The reasons for meeting in Buenos Aires are: (firstly) Clive is following up a lead for a magazine feature he's writing on the subject of Iraqi art thefts; (secondly) Argentina's devalued currency made the trip surprisingly cheap; and (finally) the city is far enough away from both their families for open privacy.

That's why I thought I might describe the rain and darkness

They can't see the city outside it could be any city anywhere

Tears sperm vaginal mucus streaky like the rain and darkness

Particularly when it's dark and raining but I thought I might because of all the rising precipitation here

This is obvious, a truism

It either fits too well or not at all

Novelists should never attempt to describe the weather

As they trundle into the rain outside the airport, two sleeveshirted men squabble for the right to porter Viv's small case. Clive rejects the hustle with a quiet uplifted palm. New to portering and bashful or maybe not too desperate, neither man insists: a single bag isn't worth the two or three dollar tip for the soak. A driver in his cab, pouting at infinite boredom, flinches out of inertia as Clive and Viv approach the curb, and dashes out into the rain, for the door, the trunk.

Popped. Dim trunk. Rusty empty wheel cache, bungee wires coiled at the ends with hot pink pliable hooks, a rough grey carpet crumby with thick dustflecks. Clive hefts up Viv's luggage and rumbles it down. Trunk slams with a catched thud.

—No really, how are we going to stop thinking about

But Clive doesn't hear because of slamming his door, and turning to catch his seat belt which isn't there while turning to tell the cab driver the number and street, and listening to a swift paragraph of Spanish not one syllable of which he understands, and replying *si*, and the cab driver saying *Palermo*, and replying *si si*.

They simultaneously realize that the reason the smell of pine trees overpowered the air conditioning and fumed fuel of the airport is the memory of their nakedness on a bed of moss and rust needles.

Viv	*Clive*
Where are you taking me?	
	I rented an apartment in Palermo for us.
Is that where everybody goes?	
	Everybody, yeah.

The cab twisting with a velocitous thrust and a nearby low car horn blaring into and out of the traffic matrix scares them like children as they flush onto the main and crowded and flowing highway. The cab driver quickly crosses himself. For what possible reason, Viv and Clive wonder together before their minds swerve apart.

The car lurches, lurches, stands still for passive traffic, and the idea of small talk would be an offence to the grandeur of the collapse they're undergoing, like sickening sea round scum rocks reduced to pools of cool slime and miniature crawling, and the end is doldrums and silence.

And into that silence

TIM

O Tim, Tim, Tim, Tim, Tim

TIM

Everybody knew about Viv and Tim. Their happiness altered rooms. They were constantly making small gifts of themselves unto one another, like bits of news or chocolate bars or oral sex or kisses on the forehead or half-minute long back rubs or shared memories. Anybody could see the mingle of need and want, habit and surprise, in Viv and Tim.

Nobody knew about Clive and Tim. When men have known each other a long time, they no longer need shared interests or even affection. A primordial, Neanderthal loyalty permeates their silence. Like the wheels of a bicycle, one moves when the other moves.

At Viv and Tim's wedding—in the spring, on the lake, Clive as best man—one of Viv's cousins, a little seven year old with his little hands in his little suit-jacket pockets, walked up to the three of them at the head table and asked "How do you kill a circus?" "I don't know, how do you kill a circus?" The cousin savored the before-punchline. "You go for the juggler." All three of them, laughing, knew—were smart enough to know—that this was the happiest. The kid walked off straight-faced.

North she ventured, far far from the world of men and women, to her uncle Phil's cabin on Lake Whiskyjack in Quebec, to write a collection of short stories about her experience of being adopted. Later she told everyone that Tim was the only procrastination she could find out there, in the wilderness. The neighbouring townspeople spoke a clotted French that neither of them could understand despite twelve years of bilingual education. Every Saturday a truck hollering up the dirt track ran civilization up and down their spines

HOW VIV MET TIM

but on Sundays nothing smoothed them out again. They were the only people on the lake for all of May and June and the trail around the edge of the water was too narrow for avoiding neighbours. She was a writer, she told him. He was an ornithologist. Studying three families of ducks breeding on Lake Whiskyjack. Barrow's goldeneye, a rare and endangered bird. Preparing a monograph on their fighting tactics and breeding practices. The drakes sometimes attack underwater, that was what was so interesting. To defend their eggs. Barrow's goldeneye lays its eggs in tree holes inland. They fight for ownership of the lake to defend their mates' food supplies. The first night Viv heard all about it over a dinner of Cheerios and bacon. She had seen ducks on the lake. She didn't know the ducks were rare. The next morning she found an envelope with three feathers tucked inside: one black, one white, one purple. The colours of the Barrow's goldeneye. If Tim and Viv were a country, the colours of their flag.

Sure, they both lived in Montreal in the early nineties and attended a Neoplatonism class together at McGill and they were both friends with a girl named Olivia, so they drifted in and out of the same parties, and they both lived in the Greek part of town, so they sometimes shared rides home. A larger, vaguer explanation than these wafts of chance was necessary—perhaps that Clive, born to factory workers in rural Ontario, aspired to Tim, whose family owned an Emily Carr and a small Rubens and both city and country homes, and that Tim, born to factory owners in Toronto, aspired to Clive, who had understood from the age of six the proper way to gut a deer.

HOW CLIVE MET TIM

Their friendship began April 17, 1996. Clive and Tim had finished their course work the night before and, to celebrate, climbed the two hundred and eighty steps or so up Mount Royal to Saint Joseph's Oratory. They arrived breathless, speechless. Brother Andre's heart sat in a small glass box in a small empty room in an enormous silence. His atria and ventricles displayed the stem of his aorta like a rubbery bonsai branch. And in the huge oratory below, prosthetics and crutches of the miraculously healed squatted in broken, holy, glorious piles.

Clive remembered Tim talking to a friend in college who watched a lot of porn and the guy said do you watch porn and Tim said no and the guy said you should and Tim asked can you recommend any that are well-made.

Solitudes

He brought her purple, black and white feathers so she brought him a peach pie so he brought her a tin bowl full of blooming trilliums so she knit him a purple wool scarf which he never wore, so he brought her a dead owl, which she buried.

Half his penis down her mouth fit searchingly. The feel of the hard rib-like veins against her wet lips up and down. Underpump of the *corpora cavernosa* on the muscle of her tongue. The tender scrotum in her fingertips and the pubic scraggliness around her hooped palm.

On a bed of salacious moss, thick with pine air, Viv and Tim lay down into the so soft scurrying of a muskrat or a porcupine on the fallen, deadened limb of a season tossed tree. Insects carried away what time would not let rot. And the sunset swayed them toward nocturnalism, swelling their eyes with photosensitive rhodopsin, until dawn, a deer curving its neck to look, the fizz of the oriole, new buzzes of old sleepers, the grounded dew. All the light in the world.

From her desk she could see Tim's duck blind across the lake, and she found herself writing, instead of a short story collection about being adopted, a science fiction novel about a futuristic Cree state covering all of Northern Quebec. A returnee is readmitted into his Cree family after many years in the cities. She wrote it quickly because she knew nobody would want to read it except her and maybe the man in the duck blind across the lake. *Enemy of my Enemy* later became a bestseller in seven countries.

The Silences Between Young Men

There was traveling to that earthforsaken lake at the end of Quebec where those precious duck families nested. Whole days passed unexpressed.

There was that time in Rome after years without seeing each other and they saw a Vermeer on loan from the Rijksmuseum: a woman receiving a love letter.

There was silence about the war in Iraq when Clive supported it and Tim did not. There was silence about Viv's novel before its success and after.

There were the long walks in Montreal, in New York, through parks, up hills, street by street in small neighbourhoods. Without a word.

There were the two months Clive was working in Egypt and Tim was in Quebec when they didn't speak for two months. The longest ever.

There was underwater in a swimming pool, watching each other dive with noiseless crashes, their bodies legion with bubbles, beneath the blue surface of laughter.

And the waves of all those tender silences smashed on the terrific emptiness at the core of Tim's madness. Tim's eyes sucked inward like voided pinpricks and his mouth was a darker abyss, a hacked-out horror smearing the silence. That's how Clive understood his friend's madness. He lost his mind with his silence.

Rooms and Premonitions

Say that all the other men in Viv's life had brought something into her room – a multicoloured quilt comforter or salt and pepper shakers or a blackboard with multicoloured chalk or a dishwasher or a lump of shit – If that's what all the other men in Viv's life had carried with them into her self, then Tim had knocked down a wall

so light and space and rain had flooded down and the things in her room, all the objects accumulated from the people she had known became encrusted with the life outside, with beautiful lichens and molds. And then he had built a long dark hallway to nowhere.

The vulnerability in Tim's close-set juniper-blue eyes had always been pronounced, as if a painter matched the tone of Tim's pupil with the crease of his hair, and arranged the shades of teeth and eyeballs to capture an impression of disturbed stillness in the slight imbalance of the pose. The fear had always been in him, always.

She had entered his rooms too. The wide-eye round tree holes where the goldeneyes laid their small tender eggs. His family's luxurious house in the country, where his parents managed to pretend that everything in the world was doing just fine and everyone, everyone who counted, everyone lucky, lived as they did, in a large country estate with a small lake and a house designed by a disciple of Frank Lloyd Wright. Then dark bars, the divier the better, with Clive, fun and strange booze. All these rooms, as distant as continents, were the same room with Tim in them.

Dinner Among Friends

Three years ago, they had all celebrated *Enemy of My Enemy* making the bestseller list in Finland at a French restaurant in Toronto, where they devoured snails and horse steak and little chocolate tarts with apple brandy. Clive was dating Emily from *The Star* then, a city desk reporter who had a Master's degree in theatre and a big round ass. Viv loved Emily and Clive, and Tim loved Emily and Clive loved Viv and Emily loved Viv and Tim. It was that kind of night. Bottle tumbled after bottle—the wine tasted like winter strawberries— until they stumbled out into the empty market in which the restaurant nestled, and even Tim was singing All Together Now (all together now) All Together Now.

Two months ago, mid-January, Clive paid a visit to Tim in the facility.* Viv ate with them. Tim stared out of his anti-psychotic daze. White bread baloney sandwiches with Cranapple juice boxes and lime Jello. The plates and cutlery were all plastic for a reason.

* "Difficulty" would be more accurate than "facility."

Again the blare of a veering car, and the scare shunts Viv and Clive from mixed memory.

❧

Viv asks the fundamental, only occasionally interrupted question of *homo sapiens*: "Where are we going to eat tonight?"

"You're hungry."

"I could eat a baby."

Clive sighs. "The daycares don't open until morning. Or you could pick off a stroller in the park."

"Anything with blood. Tonight."

❧

Again the cab driver crosses himself—they must be passing a church, Clive thinks, he must cross himself at every church— and now you can see architectural silhouettes impressing and twisting and vanishing in the middle distance against the horizon. Through the scrim of the rain, Viv catches snatches of the dramas in passing car chambers: A stony-faced beauty, thirty-six thirty-seven, near tears, smoking a grimy cigarette down to the tip. Two brothers in straw cowboy hats bouncing and punching and joking. A secretarial superfatty staring through pig glasses. Passing and receding.

❧

"You didn't eat in Atlanta then?" Clive thinks to ask.

"Tried to sleep."

"I want to take you to this place just down the street but it opens at nine. Everything here opens at nine."

✿

An old man, poised as a finance minister, desperately maintaining dignity. A group of girlfriends shaking dangling earrings to the break and beat of the bass. A handsome olive-complexioned restaurateur either cursing a hands-free cell or venting an internal furious monologue he can no longer suppress. Passing and receding and fading and reappearing.

✿

The question begins as queasiness in Clive's guts, impelled upward, unstoppably, but it only trickles out, half-choked: "How's Tim?"

"Tim? That crazy bastard? He's the detective who realizes he himself committed the crime. Like an O. Henry bit but more sappy. Some unbelievably shitty undergraduate film script."

"Nothing's changed, then."

"We are still married," Viv says.

"You know that's not what I meant."

"And then he can't prove it! That's the twist. He knows he's guilty but no one will let him bring in the criminal. That's not even that bad as plots go. But we are still married. Tim and I."

✿

"Is he still at Newmarket?"

"You want to keep me on topic. You worry about me. You worry about this weekend. How you're going to stand it."

Macktruckblare.

❧

A tough widow with a lattice of black lace veil over her pewter storm of hair. A dusty middle-aged glazier, as exhausted as the twentieth century. A young mother, glance to the rear-view mirror, fear. Passing and receding and fading and reappearing.

❧

"I cover over everything with stupid jokes and tepid anger. You know that," Viv says.

"Forgot."

"You, you don't say anything. Didn't you interview a Prime Minister once? I know what your cop out would be too. That you don't know what to say. Pure cop out. Isn't that what you'd say?"

"I can't say."

"Ranters and listeners. The two tribes of the Journalist. You want it to be all about what you're not talking about."

"I interviewed Ehud Barak but it was before he became Prime Minister."

"Listening. The Listener. That's why you love Tim."

❧

Clive is running his mind over the contours of the idea that he's in love with the woman beside him. Viv stares at the highway median which is running like a concrete ribbon being dragged beside the car until it ends with a flick of the wrist.

❦

"I haven't had much conversation lately, you can imagine. With Lithium boy. You know what I've noticed when I'm at the coffee shop or the laundromat or whatever? Because that's basically my human contact now. How many times we use the word 'crazy' or derivatives thereof. 'How was your day?' 'Insane.' 'So then the cop gave me a ticket,' 'That's crazy.' And all that. Ever notice that?"

Clive shakes his head.

"I can't stop noticing now. And I can't stop using the word either, even though I know."

❦

Clive allows himself a question: Is it even possible to cheat on someone who's insane? Legally, practically, he wonders, can one commit adultery with the spouse of someone who is *non compos mentis*? Does it technically make sense to lie to a man who cannot recognize truth? Can one be lost in a city one doesn't know? Purely as an epistemological question.

❦

They are now in the city, and the drama of other people adds flashes of passerby scenes to the melancholy isolation of men and women alone in cars with nothing but their faces. A dog-walker with a brood of a dozen leashed in a bundle. A short skirt with crossed stripe-stockinged legs sitting on a bench at the edge of a pond, smoking. A short woman running with twins in a stroller. All these people from another place, from here.

❧

Tim's far far away. Gypsy histories are blank pages. At gypsy funerals they pour cigarettes and wine and coffee in the graves. Accurate ritualists. The jumbo jets will never jumbo enough for us. Pelagic, peregrine. Lost and found and lost and found in cardboard boxes in airports all over.

A recent article in *The New York Times*, describing the collected research of a half dozen of the world's top physicists, revealed that if we had happened to exist on earth a mere five billion years ago or a mere hundred billion years in the future, we would not be aware of the dark matter which so ridicules our knowledge right at the moment. Ignorant of our ignorance, we would be obsessed with the number 6, the number of galaxies which would then be apparent to us.

Unknown Unknowns

Clive and Viv are separately and suddenly considering how madness is so fascinating in theory, with its otherness and its mercurial liminality and so on, and yet is so, so boring in practice, with its spinning wheel in a rutted track, its muddles not mysteries.

The dogwalker, the strollerpusher, the widow, the glazier, the young mother, restaurant owner, finance minister, the oblivious girlfriends, the secretary, the rural brothers, the smoking beauty, if they had so much as glanced at the taxi, would have caught what appeared to be two married melancholics bored with their bodies, passing and receding and fading and reappearing, remembering.

THE MAD SCENE No one could tell them why. Explanations reserved themselves; approached with the coolest hand, insight shied. Tim was supposed to give a lecture at an ornithological conference that day, the culmination of his years of research on Barrow's goldeneye. Stressful, OK. But the paper had been prepared and in his desk for over a month and he was going to meet his mother for lunch after giving it, that's how relaxed he was. Clive happened to be visiting—could that have mattered? He had flown in from Cairo two days before and was sleeping on the couch in their apartment. There was one other thing: they had all smoked pot the night he arrived. Laced?

Viv left Tim sleeping at eight-thirty for a meeting with her publisher. Clive, drowsing on the couch, thought he remembered Tim traipsing through the room, leaving for the conference. Then the next three hours vanished. Tim never arrived at the conference. His mother, Simone, happened to be early for lunch and found him waiting, no one could say for how long, and the moment his eyes met hers, Tim began sobbing, sobbing wildly. When at last he quieted down in his mother's arms, he begged her in whispers to take him to the police station so he could confess.

Tim wrote her. For my endless guilt, I will be punished. He told her it was like a black hole. A night chasm. Omphalos.

At the moment his best friend's mind was shipwrecking, Clive was on his knees in a small apartment on College Street trying to sodomize Diane Kim. A cliché of gorgeosity, Diane, a fucking bartender for Chrissake, with long black hair, stained in streaks like rust, rapturing the smooth Koreanness of her face, perfectly rounded nostrils, knuckle-up cheekbones, her breasts poking their chestnut nipples at the fulcrum of low crescents like the breasts in seventies honey-tinted pornography, her waist like a Hokusai wave, her hips jutting like boy elbows. She must have read about the anal craze in a glossy magazine but OK. He dared. After much and much, his fingertip, then thumb, dared explore. But when she wreathed his penis in an ugly smelling lube, and kissed him quick on the lips then slowly leaned, bent over the bed, palms on the floor, at once all the blood in his cock flooded back into his abdomen, wilting squashily. At that moment, his cellphone demurred.

Tim wrote her. Swallowed by darkness, the intestines of my soul twisted inside out. The whole world smashed like a dropped Christmas bulb on my attic floor.

"Viv?"

"Hey Simone, how are you?"

"Well I'm in the hospital, with Tim."

"You're about to tell me that everything's all right and I shouldn't worry because he's going to be fine, right?"

"I don't know, Viv darling. He believes he's committed all these crimes."

Viv could see how it made sense the way it made no sense. Tim always had frayed edges. Remembered broken glances. A too longish pause in the middle of a conversational flurry. The silences. Silences were always very Tim. The mysteries of his person aligned in constellations of pain perfected.

Simone's calm was numbed agony, a goldfish circulating through a murky fishbowl, but she was studiously gracious when introducing Viv to Dr. Radaloa, who murmured what sounded like the usual murmurs about how well the patient had calmed, and that there were solid reasons for hope, but that the situation was still very serious. The nurses in the psych ward were blackly hilarious, taking their jobs like some moderately laughable combination of hospitable compassion and sitcom slapstick. Other inmates sat in corners of a communal living room reading or watching television or eating meals off trays the same shade as the muted pink walls. Three of them: a cochineal-tressed punk princess with bandaged wrists, a carpenter (so a nurse said) with his visiting wife and two young sons, a young guy in a suit jacket who looked almost exactly like Tim.

Tim shuddering. The fear in his eyes like a creature out of his element. Fish on a slab in a Chinese restaurant or a catapulted lion. He seemed embarrassed to have lost his mind, like a man who's misplaced his wallet when the cheque's arrived.

The room was the colour of the carnation on a can of evaporated milk, a drab pink infused with drab gray. A bare bed, without frame, unchaperoned by night tables, occupied the far corner of the room. A dresser without knobs guarded the door which was never completely closed. Behind bars a diamond grill gridded the sky's humanizing blue and cloud.

"How you doing, Tim?"

"It's my friend Clive."

"Viv called me."

"Viv called you."

"What happened, man?"

"I need you to do me a favour. Can you do me a favour, Clive?"

"Anything."

"I need you to call the police and tell them where I am."

"Can I ask you why?"

"I raped. I murdered. Hundreds of people. And children."

Tim's madness climbed and abyssed, lightened and darkened, shuddered and calmed and shuddered. He believed that he had committed terrible crimes against unidentifiable women and children (nothing more specific) and later he believed that he had poisoned the lake and his families of Barrow's goldeneye had died, and later he believed that he was making the rain deadly and the air smoggy and that he was extinguishing life all over the planet.

On the fifth night, Sandy and Simone made Viv go home to sleep as if she kept sleep in pills in her bathroom cabinet (she didn't yet). The apartment was waiting for Tim. The sofa was waiting for his back and thighs. The coffee table was waiting for a water glass. The books up on their shelves were waiting for his gaze, every page in every book. The bed upstairs was waiting for the curl of his side. The streets outside their window blazed with grubby cruelty.

TIM(E)

Bouts of false hope diluted the drudgery, the promise of stability from which a leap to sanity might be attempted, and the drug regimes with their six month pickups ended in despairs as rich as whipped shit, until Viv lost any sense of what a small victory might mean, and she learned to hate even the names of the chemicals: Assoverheadandol. Catastrophix.

Six months later, Sandy, Simone, Viv and Doctor Radaloa all agreed that it was best for Tim to move to a facility near Newmarket, where his spiraling rants and swandiving depressions could be overseen by professionals at long term care. A miserable admission: The loved one's soul would not be uncrumpling like a rolled-up paper ball.

(E)MIT

On Clive's second visit to the Newmarket facility (he was returning this time from Syria), Tim took him for a walk along the edge of the facility's fifteen-foot brick wall. "I destroyed the lake," Tim told him. "I killed all those birds, all those beautiful birds that were put under my dominion." "How did you do it?" Clive asked. Tim's brow delved with concentration. "I don't know." They passed silently under the shadow of an oak which dangled a small limb from the other side of the wall. "I can climb over that," Tim said. "It doesn't look like it, but if I run up the wall and jump, I can just make it. And there's a real river over there. Wild. The opposite of in here." Clive and Tim paused, just to listen to the faint bubble and run of the rivulet on the other side of the wall. Like old times, like their old silences. Clive recalled the one class they shared in university. "Do you remember Neoplatonism, Tim?" "I do." "Do you remember the line, the line between opinion and truth?" "Yeah. There were four bits, right?" "I think you're in opinion." Tim seemed to consider. They were sitting on the lawn. He was playing with a handful of yellow grass. "I think I'm off the line."

For two years, Clive and Viv commiserated about the latest alignments of Tim's agony constellations, the fresh poses of the madness, the latest doomed strategies, and Clive, now in Baghdad, now in Kandahar, now in San Francisco, now in Cape Town, called every Sunday, visited at the last minute whenever he could. Viv loved his chatter, loved his elsewhereness and his thereness. Clive loved Viv.

Then Clive was visiting again, and went out walking with Viv— this was in Newmarket— and because Tim was shaking from his latest round of meds and needed to sleep, they went out along the brick wall, so high and formidable, and Clive showed her where Tim said he could climb the wall, and how Tim had said there was a river on the other side, a wild river, and Viv cried, and Clive asked why she was crying, and Viv said because Tim had never told her about the river, and Clive held her, and she held Clive, all that lovely warmth, and Clive pulled her away into a stand of pines and that insistent, pungent smell of pinesap, unexpected and unasked for, the smell of the strength of life in all seasons.

TIME

For two years Viv lived without. Without his body beside hers in bed. Without gossip over takeout. Without anniversary presents. Without walks. Without talks. Without back rubs. Without baths. Without the old kind of sex or the new kind of sex. Without writing a word except long, loopy emails to Clive, who always wrote back within hours, whether he was in Sweden or Kenya or Australia.

Viv lay back on a pillow of moss ebbing away from the sex with Clive, and the beginning of a good idea for a story fluttered to her forehead: an eighty-three year old woman who takes a twenty-seven year old lover. Alive again.

(*Approaching the apartment in Buenos Aires.*)

Viv
Alive again.

Clive
What's that?

Viv
It would be really great, I mean really great, if you could
make me feel alive again. A little.

(*She means yes, she means night in a new city, risk and reward, the fat pump of thick blood up the slim neck, the stirring strength of hands, she means yes yes yes.*)

The car clutches seizing spluttering rolls through a traffic circle and they can both see, in its centre, as the cab curves, revving again around it, the leaping spirit of some dead revolutionary, embronzed, on horseback—some old overturner of worlds whom others loved enough, despite his self-love, to build a monument in the middle of a traffic circle where his name could be forgotten in rust streaks and parakeet shit and the scourges of diesel fumes. Like sunset over her blood, exhaustion settles on Viv like a century's worth of disillusionment, diesel fume and parakeet shit. Like clouds breaking, Clive's anxiety startles like the idealistic horseman underneath, always rising up frozen in time and space.

The driver cruises slowly, halts, crawls forward, searching with his philosopher's face for the numbers on the elegant, corrupted building fronts. The pavements are wide and their surfaces chaotic. If a stretch runs smooth like laid marble, the next will be crushed stone cracked with weeds and the next poured concrete. The driver queries in Spanish, a number. Clive replies *si*.

Viv

Going to have to lie down. Must not have managed even the five hours I thought in Atlanta.

Clive

You know I brought some bread. Bread and wine. We don't have reservations.

Viv

No, no. I won't be able to sleep even though I'm tired. I know it. The same reason I couldn't sleep in that hotel room in Atlanta.

Clive

Have a little lie down. We'll walk to the restaurant maybe. Either that or a taxi. I'll call. If it's still raining. We'll walk. If it's raining.

The cab brakes. On the street two laughing boys chasing a balled soda can, their cheeks smudged with city, plump mothers hollering behind them. Clive has always believed that when you pay a cab, you're standing in the presence of many beginnings and many endings. Therefore tip.

Then shaking off the moist in the cold brass and expensive foyer and waiting for the elevator not saying a thing

And they don't look at the streets while the rain softens the ashes the garbage the poor whom we should think of but do not

The quick strides to the glass door the fumbled key

As Clive lifts Viv's suitcase from the trunk while she stands tense on the curb

Only a few dribs and transparent drabs splash their backs

It looks like it's about to clear up anyway it could be just the dripping from trees or eaves

I won't mention the rain again

How Did These People Arrive in This Place?

Viv was adopted by two lawyers who divorced when she was twenty, at which point she decided to search out her birth mother, a woman named Shirley McGrath. Shirley, enormously obese, lives with her three kids, all younger than Viv, in a desperate house smelling of flypaper and lobster in a small town of a thousand or so on the South Shore of Nova Scotia, where the only industry is a fish processing plant, but which Viv kept visiting until Shirley started repeatedly asking for money. Then Viv, confusing bookish with adult, left to write a short story collection about her adoption which turned into *Enemy of My Enemy* at her uncle's cabin on Lake Whiskyjack, and there she met Tim, and she met Clive through Tim, and she married Tim, and Tim went insane, and she visited Clive who was in Buenos Aires because he was working on a story there, and he met her at the airport, and they drove here.

Clive was the fourth of five brothers, born in a small town near Barrie, Ontario, where all his other brothers ended up shoveling dust at the particleboard factory. The summer after grade eleven, Clive found a job taking care of the speedboat at a wealthy country resort, where he organized the pot and hid the booze for the rich kids spending the season with their parents. Pretending friendship, they asked him where he was going to university, and he straight away said McGill because one of his cousins had gone there, and from that point, out of basic pride, he had to go to McGill. At McGill he studied the Middle East and learnt Arabic, so when he graduated the Associated Press offered him a job in Cairo, and while he was with AP, he sold a series of freelance pieces to *The Globe & Mail* and *The Boston Globe*. His big break was a 7,000 word article on Kurdistan for *The New York Times Magazine* two months before the invasion of Iraq. Then Clive heard the story of a very rich man in Buenos Aires who owned a piece of art stolen from the Iraqi National Museum, and *The Atlantic Monthly* agreed to buy the article if Clive interviewed the owner, and Viv followed him to Buenos Aires, and he picked her up from the airport, and they drove here.

the   door   jerks   shut

the   door   shudders   open

and   slow   and   stop

up   the   six   floors

and   the   elevator   levers

while   the   pulleys   pulls

her   labyrinths   and   palms

and   grip   in   labyrinths

for   her   spider   fingers

his   spider   fingers   wait

along   his   steady   arm

she   aligns   her   arm

on   Clive's   rugged   shoulder

she   lays   her   head

Viv   moves   halfway   across

the   room   shifts   up

old fashioned push buttons

it's   six   floors   up

the   door   shudders   shut

the   door   jerks   open

"Whatever that means."

"No, no, just half an hour. I like
to sleep before I eat."

"Too tired for out?"

"I'm going to have to lie down."

The Apartment

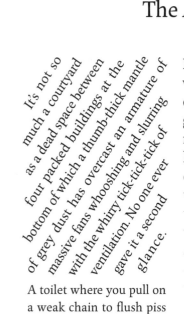 It's not so much a courtyard as a dead space between four packed buildings at the bottom of which a thumb-thick mantle of grey dust has overcast an armature of massive fans whooshing and slurring with the whirry tick-tick-tick of ventilation. No one ever gave it a second glance.

In the bedroom there's a low futon with a plain pink comforter and four dented pillows, a plane near the ground on which to make experiments with bodies in space, and to lie down to sleep the uneasy sleep of men and women who delve into the thick mulch of their mistakes, to dream about trees and equestrian statues of dead revolutionaries and the drawers where their clothes, after having rubbed against their skins, will rub against each other's skins, a surface to wake up guilty on, and to stare out through the grimy green sere curtains at the muted light coming from a courtyard or wherever, wondering what's going on, here or elsewhere or anywhere.

The closet is the dark room where her things will mingle with his things.

A toilet where you pull on a weak chain to flush piss and shit and puke away. A green sink to brush the yellow scum off your teeth and the grey city off your face. A shower to wash away sweat & snot & tears & saliva come & vaginal juice blood.

The living room and dining room have joined the kitchen—discreet white tile floors and eggshell walls postered with cliché impressionistic surfaces of bridges and water and vegetation. In a corner, a recently purchased black leather couch squats with three red pillows and a huge floor vase of emerald glass more elaborate than the white trumpet lilies it contains. The dinner table is also green glass: In the centre, a bottle of white wine, baguette, and three cheeses still in the décolletage of brown wrapper. The granite countertop shows another still life: a knife and a cut lemon resting on a brown cutting board, as in the standard scene from French cinema preceding adultery. The fridge hums almost humanly and the sink drips syncopation. The overhead casts just enough light for shadow.

At the door
Will it be OK?
Will it be OK?

From their balcony, looking at the other balconies, they can see how their balcony must look from the other balconies. A barren line for clothes hanging, tiers of uncertainly loved geraniums in buckets, cabals of plastic chairs huddled around wobbly tables, rain-sticky curlicues of smeared dust. The roofs of other people's ceilings, eeried over the street.

The couch receives her rump,
the counter his leaning hip.

Should I just
take off my
clothes? Just
carefully remove
my coat and my
shirt and my
skirt and underies
and wriggle
into bed and
spread under
the covers and
tell him to get
to me? Lets
start this, lets,
lets, lets.

"Thank you."

"It's perfect-perfect, but now I'm going
to go into that bedroom and lie down
and look at the ceiling until you come
and find me in, say, an hour and we'll
go out for steaks."

"A wee lie-down."

"I bought wine when I should have bought coffee."

The wine's wasted. Only instant coffee. Won't even mention it. Story of my life. Fine cheeses and bread and wines and soda water and limes when coffee's needed.

"We could stop off for coffee somewhere. Or chocolate."

"Right."

She heads for bed, he drifts couchward, to try not to think.

Lying on the bed full of Tim
Clive steak guilt flight adultery
money rain.

Sitting with black dress sawdusty
stolen goddess betrayal Buenos
Aires love in his awkward hands.

2

Dinner at *La Cabrera*

Viv's Side

That's what you think.

I'm going to tell you

Why won't men ever
let you finish a story.

Sorry?

Overwhelmingly bubbly.

What I meant, what I meant about
Tim's parents. Tim's mother, Simone is,
listen, never did she turn to me, at the
Cold beginning to an
evening when you're
first to arrive in a
restaurant.
dying of the dying of the light, in the
mutual collapse of our lives, and say,
like, "I feel pain," or "this is what I'm
feeling" to illuminate how much she
loved him.

We would take long walks, the two of
us, in those grimy cul-de-sacs near the
centre, or the gardens at Newmarket,
and she would hand out cryptic cross-
words. "Look how yellow the grass is,
dear, the crocuses won't know when to

Clive's Side

You're going to tell me different?
Hold on

>Waiter saying something
>about water. No idea.

What kind of water?

Bubbly or flat water?

Con gaz.
That's the only Spanish I know.

>Smooth black chairs,
>brown-papered tabletops,
>good place, good and
>Argentine.

But that doesn't mean

>Empty place. Tempura of
>echoes round our voices.

[VIV ...

spring." "That murder of crows must be hunting an owl." Halfripe little phrases.

Like trying to read wallpaper.

Twenty-first century Ontario.

The privacy.

Like, I could not have grown closer to them, but it was still trying to read wallpaper.

Or like trying to read Braille, or like trying to read bodies in the dark, or like trying to read tattoos.

Say something funny.

Nineteenth century.

Makes me wonder about Sandy.

That's what I mean.

That's not what I meant but explain, please Clive, explain to her the way Mom and Dad used to talk through the dogs. "Oh, I think Tricks wants to leave." "Oh I think Tricks likes his little space in the great outdoors."

Sandy must know. He must recognize, ah, crocuses, that wistful spring in Gibraltar, ah, the crows we saw bird watching in the Arctic, ah, some elaborate code. In order to understand each other without talking to each other. Know what I mean?

I've always thought Sandy and Simone were one of those old couples
who do it a lot.

You don't relish the image.

That gorgeous photo of
my (not real) father on
a flatbed truck, his chin
frizzy, fuzzy, rawlike.
His sailors' arms
crossed over.

You embarrass at the idea of parents
having sex, child?

You're the fourth child of?

I wonder if it's because I'm adopted.
That I don't care. That I don't mind
thinking of my folks that way. Other
than the ugliness of their tired old
flesh. But maybe I put too much on
my adoption. I wonder.

And now he's an
old man. He must
be an old man now.

Ever seen a picture of your folks
when they were young? You know,
our age? And you never thought,
seeing that picture, the fun they
must have had screwing you into
existence?

Starving. I'm
desperadoically
starving.

Out the window,
a sine curve of
a beauty in a
Casablanca raincoat
curves an eyebrow
around a tucked-
No.   back strand of jet,
and passes.

My parents never had sex.

Four brothers.

More tigers in
captivity than
in the wild.

You could write a book.

Out the window, a
red Porsche wraps
No and no. Is that what you thought   around the corner
with Shirley?   like a shawl.

His devastational smile.

Shirley weighs a deuce-and-a-half easy, possibly a trey, so mechanics, not taboos were the question. And I never had any other image of my father than this gorgeous photograph where he's sitting on a flatbed truck, his chin sort of raw and frizzy with a bit of beard, arms crossed like ropes. He would have been too young for me in that photograph.

I took photographs of Tim while he was sleeping, my, that was tacky. In the mornings he would play at death and I would play at life and in the night he would be life and I would be death. Swallowtail coats. Swallowtail butterflies. Swallowtail fret moulding.

You must have been out to Swallowtail.

The country place.

Swallowtail.

It's the shape of the building. The way the two wings arch and sweep around the pond and then curl a tad at the edges.

Pick a fold and fuck
it. Sexist or do they
like it? Almost a
compliment.

All this time we're
glancing down at
the menus without
reading them.
Unknown langauges.
Funny little rituals.

I know what you mean about Sandy
and Simone though. No separate
bedrooms for them.

Sorry?

I didn't know it had a name.

I don't remember any

Imagine my brothers
at that place.
That one time A.J.
borrowed a .50 cal
from his buddy Brett
and we shot up that
dumped rustbucket
Chevy from, like, a
mile away.

[VIV…

Out the window,
a resigned baby
strapped into a
cheap stroller plays
with the fringes of
the recently unpeeled
plastic cover.

I didn't know until Simone told me. I
don't know if Tim even knew, or knows.
Even knows.

Kinda sexy waiter.
Bends from the waist.

No.

But I am starving.

I should have

The first time I went out there, I remember, I kept thinking about my
brothers. My family owns a place up
North, the real North. Doesn't have
a name or a shape. But my brothers. I
remember looking at this little slough
Tim's parents were so proud of and
thinking about my brothers, drunk as
bishops, with loaded rifles, you know,
sniping off the mallards, and oh

Lone waiter again.
Overturning our
glasses. Wondering
gracias.   aloud to himself
whether we're
ready. Only city I've
ever visited where
No, no.   nobody speaks any
English. Nobody.
We're not ready right?   Better ask her but
she must be hungry,
she told me she was
No gracias.   starving.

[VIV...

A book about an 80-
year-old woman with
a 30-year-old man
(82/28 for symmetry)
and they barely speak
the same language.
She says "drunk as a
bishop" and he says
"What? What are
you saying?" Burning
to make sense of
each other.

Right.

Right.

You order then. Order and then finish
your story.

I'm starving. Finish.

Dank and amphibious
odour of degenerate
regeneration.

OK let's decide what to eat.

We're eating steak.

Bloody succulent mopped by powdery potatoes.

Not baby.

The one advantage of coming so early is the service.

The pond at you call it Swallowtail?
My brothers. First time, I remember
walking along the hallways staring
at the walls and forgetting about that
pond they were so proud of. They
seemed, like, so dazzled by the nature, and I was thinking the parents of
a friend of mine own an Emily Carr.
They own Group of Seven paintings,
you know. And I had never seen anything like it.

She told me she was starving two hours ago so why didn't she eat bread and cheese in the apartment?

[VIV...

Yes, I am doomed,
to one thing or
another. Hidden
fate, oldest story.
Your end is prepared
but in such a way
you can never
figure out what it
is. The universe as
sleight-of-hand man.
Surprise! At my
wedding I thought I
would end up with
Tim forever but here
I am in a resto in BA
all moist for the best
man.

The money.

See you do speak it.

When you were at Swallowtail, did Sandy
ever show you the bottle cap collection.

Not another short
story. Sick of short
stories.

It's an immaculate collection.

It's cute.

The world. That world.

Si, un mollejas,

un lomo, sangue,

un ensalada verde,
e esto Malbec,

una botella.

Gracias.

Trust me no.

Smooth-shaven waiter again, repeated attempts at ordering in Spanish out of what he thinks is accommodation. Spanish isn't rocket surgery, and you're still just a waiter.

The bottle cap collection!
For hours and hours.

Your great grandfather and your grand-father and your father amass art and books. You collect bottle caps.

Oh yes, I love the bottle cap collection. Always wanted to talk about the bottle cap collection.

[VIV...

Out the window,
street corner.
Any street corner.

I have such trouble imagining you as
a child.

You're such a patient beast. You're
such an attentive, calm, unperturbed
in the shadows, taking down little
notes. It's hard to see you in a house
full of particle board factory workers.
It's impossible for me to see you in,
like, a small town. Restless, born in an
airport, you know. Bored if you're not
in the air. Hard to see the child.

Out the window, three
sparrows land, fluff, find
no seeds, flutter off.

Yeah?

And other people.
Mother with children.
Father later? Or none?

Tim must have told you

I collected bottle caps when I was a
kid. And then I grew up.

Look. More people.
Save us from our
emptiness.

Why?

Viv's sensitive face,
her big-toothed smile,
her uncomforting
sense of humour. The
title of her first pony
book written at the
age of eight, Tim told
me, was "Ariella and
the Fields of Mercy."

I think I can imagine your childhood.

I think I can. Ballet classes. You're not
the best but you're the most popular.
You have been known to make de-
liberate missteps. At school, you re-
fuse to follow trends. Straight As. You
wrote your first book when you were

I wonder if Tim told
him I was a bully too,
like when I took Rosa
out and gossiped about
her and broke her poor
little heart, and if I have
a daughter she'll be
punished for the sins of
the mother but that's
her surprise. In the
future, surprise! The
past you didn't know
about. Not even your
past! It's your mother's!
Surprise! The oldest
story.

You must have been an unnerving
boy.

I was a bully. I should have been
smacked right across my fat little ass.

I once convinced everyone in my
class to give the silent treatment to
a girl named Rosa until she left the
school. Which she did. Her parents
took her. Because of me.

A bad bitch, I was. Grotesque.
A grotesquerie.

I wonder what those
Buddhists felt when the
Taliban bombed the
Afghan idols. Aren't
they supposed to
accept?

eight. About a pony. You have one
close friend. Elaborate stories in your
head.

Sipping frizzy water.
Touching cutlery
and tabletop and
lap. Then folded
hands. Staring out the
window: a workman
walking with his
toolboxes over his
back away from us
and home.

I was nervous.

Like what?

You almost sound proud.

When she's upset,
Tim told me, she
reads. Like when her
parents divorced or
meeting her birth
mother. Twelve hour
stretches of Dickens.
Every Greek tragedy
in a month. Then
when it's all over, she
writes. Funny.

[VIV...

Anyway. Tell me about the story
you're working on.

Who's it for?

You've never written for them before.

He wrote that huge
embarrassing piece
supporting the Iraq
war for *The New York
Times Magazine*.

Right.

You said it's a figurine.

Sixth millennium?

Jesus.

The figurine story.

The Atlantic Monthly's interested.

No and it's not a commission yet.
They think, and I agree with them,
that I can't write this story without a
photograph of the artifact or without
talking to the owner, Chicas-Rendon.

The artifact itself is great, and I'll
have a complete portrait of the Baghdad Museum Project and I've interviewed three looters, though not the
guys that stole this piece. But I need
Chicas-Rendon.

It's an alabaster statuette from the
sixth millennium BCE.

Eight thousand years old.

I know. I think the article will be, like,
a history of a penny thing.

She's thinking of
that article I wrote
supporting the war.
Blair mentioning
Baldwin quote. One
to talk.

quote-unquote

Eight thousand year
old alabaster figurine
of a mother-goddess
excavated from Tell
es-Sawwan.

[VIV...

He lives in Damascus,
Baghdad, Cairo,
Montreal, wherever
the mess is, trying
to forget he's from
a small town near
Barrie but he can't,
he can't.

Sounds rather fromagey that last bit.

At least they
could bring the wine.
Which will render me
drunk rapidomente.
Or maybe here wine
comes with beef.
With the meal.
Carne e sangue.
No that's Italian.

Like the Fifties O'Keefe bottle cap.

This is illegal?

Purchasing art looted from the
National Museum of Iraq?

Like, following the object over time,
over the various possessions. As a
kind of way of displacing the whole
Iraq fiasco. Like the war in Iraq is just
one moment in eight millennia if you
know what I mean.

I know, I know. It's just, like, a frame
for the moment. Dropped in the
mud. Rebirth through archeological
dig. Then the theft during the invasion. And now I have a contact with a
dealer in New York who says he's sure
Chicas-Rendon has it, I think because
the dealer sold it to him, because, like,
he said, it's quote just the kind of piece
Chicas-Rendon needs unquote.

So I've set up a meeting.

What?

Is she? Is she liking this?
I don't think she's liking
this. Is she?

Fromagey? What
does that mean?

quote-unquote
coming again.

Kind of piece of ass
Chicas-Rendon likes.
He met his future wife
Amalia at the funeral for
her husband who was
his prime competitor
in the mattress market
until then. Do people
murder for the mattress
business in Argentina?

Buried alive. Like
a stolen goddess.
Mouthful of ashes.

So why would he talk to you?

What do you think are your chances
of bamboozling this guy?

Out the window,
beauty in a Beatles
cut stares right back,
embers the tip of
her cigarette with a
cynical inspiration.

Does he even speak English?

The poor Chicas-Rendons. With
you at their throat.

Only rich people illegal. I mean nobody gets shivved in prison.

                                      "This is an urban myth."
                                      That's what Chalabi
                                      said. Wow.

This thing, the Baghdad Museum
Project, which is, like, you hand over
the stolen goods and they give you
full immunity. What I'm hoping is
that Chicas-Rendon sees that I know,
he sees there's somebody else who
told me who knows, and, basically,
freaks out. So. So I think I can get him
to give the piece up, if I arrange the
transfer. And that's my final scene.

                                      Bamboozle: nice.

His wife wants to talk, so I think excellent. Of saving him. I'm saving him,
you know.

                                      Salvageable or
                                        unsalvageable?

Chicas-Rendon ran a mattress factory
in New York for years. Owned. So,
yes, enough. But the key is the wife,
and she's listening.

[VIV...

Out the window,
businessman in blue
and gold. Cellphone.
A mafioso stride in
his walk.

Tomorrow never comes.

You should tell me that when we re-
turn to the apartment. Tell it to me
all husky like.

Out the window, a
paunchy man (mid-
forties? mid-fifties?)
smooths down
waves of Jewish hair
across his forehead
and drags his six-
year-old son, glum,
possibly spoiled,
with quarter-pleas,
quarter-threats, past
them.

So what's this statuette that Chicas-
Rendon stole?

What's it a statue of?

So, like, a fertility object?
An erotic fetish?

Eight-thousand-year-old artifacts
from Iraq. There will be no mercy.
Anyway. We'll have to see tomorrow.
Tomorrow.

Behind every great
fortune is a great crime.
Behind every statuette.
Behind every bottle cap
collection. Who said
that?

I'll remember.

Back in the apartment,
cool naked flesh. The
smell of the city fumes.
Wraiths of other
people everywhere.

What is it?

A woman.

She's hungry, fidgety.
Should I call over a
waiter? Should I?
Yes? No?

How can I forgive myself
for what I'm about to do
with you?

The most important whole other
thing.

I should have been
smacked. I should be
smacked.

No, no, it is the most important part
of the story you're trying to tell.

What is all that over though? Is it
over love? Is it over the birth of children? Or is it over the possession of
things of value? Over money?

Old paunchy man
enters restaurant.
Surprise. Speaking
French. The waiter
speaks French.
A discussion of
booster seats.

Is it over religion? Is it over the
truth? Is it over beauty, the mirror-
ing possibilities of art? What, exactly,
has drifted and wavered and sunk
and risen over these oceans of time?

Yeah right.

I don't know. I haven't gotten into all that yet. That's going to be a whole other thing.

Too polite, and what's the point. You think the waiter cares, Clive, you pathetic, unmasculine shit?

I guess.

Don't you think the readers will want to know more about the Baghdad Museum Project than about the archeology? And the looting. And the recovery. And the black market.

How wrong I may be.

Interesting.

Oceans of time: nice.

You should write it.

[VIV...

Thank Christ the wine.
Big slabs of beef next.
Patience, my pet, patience.

That depends. How much do you
not want to hear, or rather how
much do you want to hear about
nothing? I told my publisher the
other day that I may as well stash
my pens in my vag, they're just
about as useless.

Sorry I don't have another inappropriate joke with which to limn
this awkwardness, so I'll

The wine tastes nice. I'll
take you to bed. I'll grasp
you in one hand like a
dozen pencils (fourteen?).
To write whatever

-

I'm thinking about how much
Tim and I have lost, about how
much time we could have reveled
in, and the missing action.

Gracias.

How is your writing?

Don't taste it, just smell it and it's a prosperous and sophisticated wine, with tantalizing suggestions of battleships, cumulus clouds and melanoma sailing easily to a long finish of sweaty headphones and drug money. Or some such.

"Vag." O. Vagina.

No go on.

Last time I puked was from red wine.

[VIV...

Wrecked the night.
I just wanted to live
a little. Go ahead, live
a little. More wine.
More surges of wine.

Lost.

The times you don't even know
you're enjoying until you're remembering them, like, years later. Like you
can run your hand across
the texture of that time.

Do you?

Tim taking his lith now.

I wish I had no memory. I want to
forget every second of the past two
years and two months and however
many days. And however many minutes and hours. I want to
deposit them in an underwater safe
in a cave on the Abyssal plain.
That's what I'm thinking.

Oceans of time.

Do you ever think about Tim?

I want to forget him. I ache.

Tim. More brother
to me than my
brothers, a canister
of sugar, a favorite
chair, a joke you've
heard a hundred
times before but
still laugh when you
hear it. Remember
that time we met in
Rome? He looked
like a lumberjack,
wearing a red flannel
shirt in Rome. And I
was Tommy Franks.
Combat khakis.

I think I know what you're talking
about.

No.

All the time, Viv.

[VIV...

Thank Christ some dead carcass is
arriving.

And what parts of the slaughtered
magnificent beast are these morsels?

I rather prefer my afters
to my befores, said old
Granny Black.

I'm just a girl but that sounds like a
terrific cover for an outright nasty
nasty bit.

What's that?

And where is the pancreas?

Deliciousness.
Spring is Fall and
Fall is Spring. The
opposite of the world
is only a flight away.
Regeneration replaced
by degeneration or the
other way. Which
way me?

It's like a meat marshmallow.

Yes.

These are the sweetbreads.

From the kitchen door
swung open, with
glimpses of the effort
behind the pleasure,
the waiter lifts like
clouds on a wooden flat
a small mound of juicy
sweetbread lumps.

A sweetbread is a calf's pancreas.

A calf's pancreas is a sweetbread.

Inside the cow. And now on our
plates. Try.

Succulence of the new
world entire, glory,
under and over, the
sweetness of conquest,
brutal, bright America.

I love the nasty bits.

[VIV...

Listen
Sorry.

Sorry can mean many
things in Canada. It can
mean "fuck you" and it
can mean "don't blame
me for things that I can't
control," and "that was
your fault" and "I'm not
going to listen anymore."
And also, "I apologize."

I'm sorry for talking that way before.
About Tim. You know.

So what were you going to say?

Male friendships are
just so much more
substantial, aren't they?
Brother goes to the
police station to bail
out his brother who
killed their third brother.
Sister's just you're a
bitch, no you're a bitch,
no you're a bitch.

The thing about the flight

Now you go.

They ate well in Barrie, I see.

How do you like

No you, please.

Yeah.

Nothing. Overwhelmingly nothing.

I don't want to
forget him. I want
him back and to
travel with him
again. Shanghai.
Saint Petersburg.
Sierra Leone. That
goodness in his
heart.

It reminds me

I was going to say that this dish reminds me of my childhood.

We ate different.

Hunting.

Another family
coming in. Four
women, two men.
Multilingual. Babble
beginning to rumble
out the spaces of the
restaurant.

[VIV...

In my family, we ate raw fish.

It's what two lawyers catch after a
long day in the swamps, and with
nothing but their bare hands and a
platinum express card.

I envy more than
anything women in
middle life who have
close relationships
with their sisters.

He wasn't on board.

But this he would understand.
Eating pancreas.

Could be a project for him.

Moose.

Bear even.

Sushi.   Like that one time I
                                                tried explaining to my
                                                father and he asked
                                                "You mean they eat
                                                it raw?"

I'll never forget explaining sushi to my
father.

"You mean they eat it raw?"   I wonder if Dad's eaten
                                                every part of the cow?

I wonder, I wonder if he's eaten every
part of the cow. I know he's eaten ear.
I'll have to ask.

Like seeing every Vermeer in the world.   Villa Borghese.
                                                Woman with letter.
                                                Lovely

[VIV...

Let us endeavour
to make
more polite
conversation.
Let us imbibe
much more cool
ferocious wine.

Can you tell me something?

What's with you and the Middle East?

Yeah.

Your living.

You feel alive there.

The bottle's half-
finished now,
lathed by the
open air.

To a point.

Sure.

The obsession.

Everybody has a silly obsession with
the Middle East for no good reason.
It's just my profession.

Exactly.

That's an interesting word. Alive.

Boredom has many advantages. Boredom is the most underrated condition
in the world.

The firemen walk into the
World Trade Center, and
they don't know, they don't
know, they stumble around
pretending they know.

All the killers and all the
death. And the time in Tel
Aviv, twice in Baghdad.

The sight of tanks renders
one quite alive.

Buenos Aires has bombs
right? Homemade affairs
right? American banks
carting the money off.

[VIV...

Politics: Change the
subject like a polite girl.

How's Emily?

Yeah.

No.

But you

So it's not

Roger.

Roger Federer.

So tell me
More carcass!

The steak arrives. Flesh
stewed in its fumes and
infused with the stories
of grasses and flames,
parrots shocking up
from the pampas, the
reserved fatalistic gazes
of the endless field of
steers startled by a
shotgun blast. Life of
flesh. Vie de chair.

Let me pour you

Perfect.

So tell me

How many women have you slept with?

Emily Cole?

She's a single mom.

Poor, poor Emily.

Yeah.

Nearly three years for us.

Would I name my kid Roger Lee-Cole?

He's the only Roger I know.

Right.

Here it is.

Thanks, I'll just cut

There you go.

Out the window, two
young boys in laughter
raptures hefting
a wriggling friend
who's near tears with
impotence and anger
and sadness. Power
versus powerlessness.

Yes?

No really. Please.

Why won't you tell me?

Then tell me about Emily.

Fifty-five. Christ.
Greypubichairphobia.
Must be a proper
name for that. But
George Clooney.

No.

Ovid. Metamorphoses.
A woman turned into
a laurel tree. A woman
turned into a spider.
Material. Tim, in the fall,
we drove through New
England in the middle
of the leaves dying and
he brought a bottle of
vodka and we took a
shot every evening at
the hotel. Warmish
serpent-skin alcohol.

Hundreds and hundreds. More wine for you?

I've lost track.

I don't keep track anymore. Honestly, I've stopped with that nonsense.

Emily fell in love. Right after me. Emily fell in love with a fifty-five-year-old guy.

Yes. She fell in love with a fifty-five-year-old architect named Ovide. Ovide, as far as I could tell, manu-factured species of curvilinear vases out of computer programs. Which is not what I thought architects did. Twenty-three-year age difference. I remember that number because her birthday was May twenty-third and I was living in room five twenty-three in the hotel when we were dating. Anyway. Ovide knocked her up I think. They married after, like, six

Not again. Gorgeous steak. Poor Ovide, he'll never sliver open an Argentine steak again. If he ever did.

Bigger piece, littler piece. You will always have the poor with you.

Based on the interior symmetries of the dog rose, the English rose and the tulip.

[VIV...

I wish I were pregnant
like a magnificent vase.

You said she was a single mother.

Death?

Her fate,
surprise, surprise,
is to widowhood.

Terrible.

What do you think of that as a way
to die?

A woman turned
into a bluebird, no, a
nightingale. The desire
to be transformed.
The desire to go on
being the same. Is this
what the 82 year old
wants?

Did you ever meet him?

"Ovide"?

106

months. She was pregnant at the wedding, to which I was invited. Magnificent vases at that wedding.

You can tell by the gazes scuttled behind our eyes that we want to look inside one another.

Death.

What I heard was he had some job arranging the housing for executives at a mining site and he was surveying the plots and his helicopter crashed into a cliff face. In Peru.

Odour of copper. Memory or steak?

Yes.

I'm not sure there are any good ways to die when you have a newborn son.

He was just your standard fifty-five year old Chinese French-Canadian architect. Working in Peru.

You can tell by our elbows over the edge of the table, knees glancing around under there, banging a bit, half-intentional accidents.

[VIV...

Blood flavour conjures
the Neanderthalette
primordial mother
back up.

Fraught.

A bit like Simone.

Clive is a good man. He
is understanding, stands
under, catches the drift.

I have trouble understanding people
who don't say what they mean. Who
don't speak what they're saying.

Like the time with Simone
and the vials of heroin.
Tell that story.

I know it's a failing, I know. I remember
once in Sandy and Simone's apartment,
I went into the bathroom for something, and I found, I discovered this,
like, this little sandalwood box. And in
the box was heroin. And a syringe. So

And he was quiet. At least the couple
of times I met him. Although you felt
like he felt you, if you know what I
mean. I don't know. It was, like, "another glass of wine," meant "one may
as well indulge as one so rarely en-
counters men of our caliber in one's
daily rounds of social engagements."
Know what I mean?

Exactly.

Yeah.

You? You say whatever you want and
drop smoke bombs to escape whenever it gets dicey.

Oxford dons huff
snuff in lovely cellars
disputing the proper
use of that and
whom.

Using Ovide's pain to
squeeze Tim's wife
into bed: traitor.

You cannot serve
two masters. That
was what the
reverend Bob Dylan
said.

109

The suggestion of this boy's shoulders are strong. To hang a suit right. To hang your ankles.

I asked Simone about it, and she assembled the euphemism squads right quick, but still, she was telling me this story. This real story. And it was that Sandy's mother has been very sick and had wanted to die, and so Simone arranged the matter with the family doctor. A phone call. In the middle of the night, a package arrives in a taxi. There's a sandalwood box. And all I could think about was how she was saying, like "mother wasn't feeling very well," instead of "the old bitch was dying of cancer," and, like, "I helped her," instead of "I killed her." All I could think about was her silly dress and all I can think about now is that sandalwood box.

It's a terrible failing.

I watch all this from the outer. This is how the women see the world after they've been magicked into spider, laurel tree, nightingale. They peer out.

Dr. Radaloa called me one morning and I rushed up to Newmarket. They had found him naked under the

This woman's eyes
like poison petals.
This woman's heart
like knotted roots.

Pick a fold.

Viv.

Sudden lull in the
restaurant. No one
will ever understand
why there must be
these sudden lulls
in restaurants.
Epidemic.

[VIV...

So what happened to me? What was I transformed from and into? For what crime?

Bursting with love and I will shatter with love like a mirror staring into the head of snake's hair.

The world will have changed for this 82-year-old woman. The 28-year-old lives in a world which is the world. Or no, maybe change is so rapid no one can figure, no one can prepare. A novel about an 82-year old woman who learns to ride fate with a 28-year old man.

moon, ecstatic, rubbed himself all in dirt and flowers out in the lawn.

Tim's pantheistic moment.

They think he burst with love for all nature for a single night and then with the dawn. A phase. By the time I arrived, he had destroyed all of it, he had wrecked the rain, depilated the rain forest, extinguished the birds from the sky. Arrogant prick. It takes the whole species, all of us, working together, to do that. But I would have enjoyed seeing him ecstatic, even if only for an afternoon. I've been sentenced to death through boredom.

You know who I love? I love Paris Hilton. She's the goddess of boredom. You see that video? She's, like, bored being fucked on camera. People say she's just famous for being famous, but she represents the truth of

Remember in Rome?
The whole time Tim
ate nothing but one
McChicken sandwich at
11 am and another
McChicken at 7 p.m.
And every day he would
have a crap at three in
the afternoon, a perfect
egg-shaped crap.
Chicken before egg.

I haven't heard about this.

What happened?

No.

"You mean they
eat it raw?"

[VIV...

I wonder if I bit off a bit of
Clive's shoulder, whether
the taste would flood my
mouth like this lust steak.

the bored women of this planet. Here
she is, bored in her Benz. Here she is
again, bored in Saint Barts. Bored in
Bungalow 8. Bored everywhere ex-
pressly designed to be exciting. She
couldn't be more bored.

I felt her last year. She was practically
the only thing I was interested in. And
COPS, which is the last place you see
poor people on TV.

Enough. Take me home.
Take me to bed. Carry
me off this steak
and to bed.

So. Are you really not going to tell me
anything about your life with women?

114

... CLIVE]

The last liquid in the
bottle glugging.

A friend of mine who works at *People*
once waited three nights for her to
show up at a sushi restaurant.

And now typical
conversation stuff.
Refuge.

What's next?
More to drink.
So pour, man, pour.

I know what you want, Viv. You want
me to gossip about myself the way I
did when you and Tim were just

115

[VIV...

Out the window,
brothers squabbling
with Italianate hand
gestures about their
mother's habits.

Have you ever wondered why men
who sleep around are considered
good with women?

The restaurant is all
couples and families
and how will it seem if
we're the first to leave?
Like tourists or lovers?

You would think that a man who
settles with a single woman would be
considered good with women. 'Cause
he knows what he's doing.

Tim's gone.

Tim's not coming back.

Madness is life
and its opposite.

married. When I was the single friend, and you still wanted to live through all that shit vicariously. And it was interesting. But how could it be interesting now? It's not even interesting to me now. It's just not interesting.

Seventy-two
but who's counting.

I completely agree.

I want to buy another bottle of wine and pour it all over my body.

I agree completely.

Change subject.

So this pantheistic phase, this lunar phase Tim underwent, what did Dr. Radaloa say about it?

How gone?

When Tim rises in our hearts, a melancholy wave of unanswerable questions, a mood of imponderability, rises with him.

OK.

Don't make me fucking laugh. A bit much, don't you

An opera and then you take me to bed for private coloratura? There's no need for that. But we'll go. Complete the picture. I better not fart and wreck it.

I lost track of the world because of Tim. I haven't even been following the news. The broader world for me is what I can scan off the front pages when I'm crouched down at the bus stop. Or twenty minutes of CNN in the waiting room at the hospital.

Blood and wine and bread and water. This restaurant is fine.

It's been the same news for, like, five years now. A white courtyard, some kids in fatigues with machine guns, robed men, veiled women, scared

Change subject again.

Anyway. I thought tomorrow we
might go for a walk at the nature
reserve.

Fun weekend. Things to
do over the weekend.
Defence of tourism.
Good idea. Makes us all
smarter and more open.
Good, but who would
publish it?

And then the opera. They have a
great opera house here.

Change subject again?

We're in a mess. As a summary.

Her heart-shaped
face like a box of bad
chocolates.

[VIV...

children, stumbling, being pushed
around. Always the same story.

A mob drenched
in its own sweat.

Or a mob drenched in flop sweat.

So, so dark.

It's so dark.

Ignorance is hope. For you.

I need to write again.
An 82-year-old woman
with a 28-year-old man.
Knowable unknowable.

So, so dark.

What are we going to do?

It's always been the same story.

It's always been that story. The same story. Over and over again. War, love.

It doesn't mean.

We are completely in the dark. We have no idea. Out of this mess we're in. How? But somehow, or not, we're going to stumble out. I mean, if we weren't in the dark

There isn't any hope in what we know.

Don't know.

It's not entirely ridiculous to claim that politicians are not people.

Salim shot through the guts and head. Muhammad disappeared. Many fates worse than death. Faizal blown to Allah at the Golden Shrine. All mine, all mine, I carry them.

Out the window, nothing. No cars. Nobody.

[VIV...

I'm going to be, like, thinking about Emily now.

Emily putting her boy to sleep. She tidies the kitchen, ladles the leftover chili into the Tupperware, goes to watch a little TV, has a cry, sleeps.

Which part?

That is embarrassing.

Karta.

Einstein said something like, if you put your hand on a hot stove for a minute, it seems like two hours, but if you spend two hours with a pretty girl, it seems like a minute. Many have called him a genius.

Yeah.

You know her story reminded me of
Enemy of My Enemy.

Emily's a bit like

Embarrassing. That you can't see it.
Even more embarrassing that I can't
remember. Near the end.

Last morsels of life of the
flesh.

The main character—Corta? Karta?—
she's visiting her birth mother in the
Cree territory, and they start talking
about her birth grandmother?

Sip, not glug, of wine.

And there's that story about the grandmother having a lover in her youth
who she thought had died because he
was captured or killed or something,
then she married somebody else. And
then he shows up years later.

We're going to have
sex tonight. Funny how
you can tell these things
without being able to tell.

And this causes Karta to reevaluate all
her previous relationships, which are

No one ever understood their grandmother. And we will be misunderstood by our granddaughters. The curving of the world. The theory of relativity. No. The theory of irrelativity. OK. Now put it into a love story. With an 82-year-old woman and a 28-year-old man. How?

Right.

How did Emily remind you of Karta?

Because they were expecting him to die first.

all petty and thin. In the light of this
big old romantic affair.

Like, if she had known her proper history, would her whole idea of love
have changed? It's a great part.

Remnants of a meal.
Scarlet puddles and
messes. Sex and meals
leave messes. Insight of
waitresses and maids.

I imagine them. Emily and Ovide.
An older man with a much younger
woman. A sophisticated architect
with the crass junior reporter. This
is the story, good and bad, that they
have about themselves. Which
is shattered when the helicopter
smashes into the cliff face in Peru.

Suddenly he's the young one. When
they married it was for the flicker
of his life. But they didn't know it. If
they had known. See what I mean?

Explanation for
everything, don't ya
Clive? That's what Mom
would say. When Jeremy
was over and we were
flipping through a book,
and there was a picture
of a castle, and he asked
me what the portcullis
was called, and I said
"portcullis," and mom
whispered from the
kitchen, "explanation
for everything, don't ya
Clive?" 12 years old.

[VIV...

Language like water
pours along the surface
of curved time.

After transforms before. For Emily.
Poor Emily.

Love in the rear-view mirror. I thought
you were going to say the grandness of
love in the face of death. The grandness of the failure of love in the face of
death.

A way to talk to
Tim, a way to speak
to the mad.

"If only I'd known," "If only." That's the
lemon juice. I remember I wrote that
bit when Tim and I first started out,
and I remember thinking "I have my
big love, it's come to me, I know that
love is real, as real as a glass of water."

Poor Emily. Poor me.

Let's go to bed.

Said it. Said it at last.
So we know what
we're doing. We know
what we're going to do.

Let's finish off this charge of erotic
wine and go to bed. Enough. Enough.

126

Right.

A surprising number of
my friends are dead.

That too.

Salim's face.
Muhammad's face when
he laughed at my joke
about horseradish.

As real as a glass of water.

As real as a glass of water.
I love that. She has such a
tongue.

Dessert?

Waiter again.
Please go away.

No gracias.

Remember? In the chill of autumn, in the park five minutes from the house of my childhood bedroom, a boy named Willing Lattner stuck one, and then two fingers inside me. And then Willing Lattner placed his thumb on my clitoris. You could see the mist of our breaths in the air. It was cold.

Enough guilty memories, enough guilt, enough memories, enough waiting around in restaurants, waiting in airports in Atlanta, you know, and not touching and not writing, and hating the phone, the nightmares, and not knowing and not being anywhere.

I think I'm a week away from the doctors saying it's over. What do I do then? And Emily's got a kid. Craziness.

But I hate that word. I guess I had to say it eventually. It's unavoidable. Collecting bottle caps. Looting museums. The mind has sick wallpaper.

No more steak.
Cut loin.

Who?

Who?

Ahmad Chalabi.

Enough what?

Tim at the airport in
Montreal. We drove
North. We should have
cut open our hands and
become blood brothers
right then.

It's been impossible.

It is.

Say something funny
here Clive, funny.

Recently I've been obsessed with
Ahmad Chalabi.

If she doesn't I will reach
out my fingers and brush
along her arm.

Speaking of sick wallpaper. For a
month, like a month ago, I couldn't
get Ahmad Chalabi out of my head.

[VIV...

Out the window, a
woman angrily peeling
an orange while
walking home late
from the office.

That's whacked.

W-W-A-C-D.

Did you ever meet Trish Beaulieu?

I suppose there's no reason you should
have. I knew her in residence and she

It doesn't matter I suppose. Anyway,
Trish had a lot of fantasies about having sex with Jesus Christ.

Repeated fantasies. I wonder honestly
if it's uncommon because she grew up
in a fundamentalist home, where all
these pictures of Jesus hung on the
walls—you know the one, that, like,
soft white guy with cloud curly chin
fuzz and that shoe salesman smile. It
makes sense right? The best looking

The empty wine bottle
stands in the middle of
the table like a tower
waiting to crumble.

Obsessed. Rivetted to his shitty little
soul. I would find myself, like, wondering what to do about something,
and asking "What would Ahmad
Chalabi do?"

Sorry?

Yeah.

No.

The restaurant set like
the bridges of New
York, tension lines and
everything in between.

Jesus.

Nailing Our Lord
to the Cross.

She appalls me. So good
to be appalled again. It
reminds me of when I was
young and good.

131

[VIV...

With his cunning,
collapse-proof.

guy around. It must be nice to have a
god you can take to bed. Like the
statuette from Iraq.

That he was a god in bed?

He was in the air.

Should have said
"afflict" shouldn't I?

I must say he didn't inflict me. I think
more of

I think Bush and Laura must be one of
those couples like Sandy and Simone.

I like that.
Sexual phantom.
Sexual wraith. Worth
stealing. 82-year-old
woman visited by the
ghost of her 28-year-
old husband.

All the time.

People said that about Clinton.

Entered their dreams. No one ever said
anything, all in the mess of it, about
Clinton being one way or the other.
Which is revealing. But earlier, in the
first election, after Gennifer Flowers.

Like a phantom. Like, like a sexual
wraith.

It's in the sidelights of our
minds that the crowd
speaks no English, which
means we're talking
louder, listening less,
falling more quickly,
deeper.

Afflict.

At it.

I bet the President of the United
States and his wife are subject to a
rigid schedule. Intercourse three times
a week. Monday night, Wednesday
morning, and Saturday afternoon.

The blood of the flesh
and the crush of the grape
have flooded, glutted our
guts, our brains, our veins.

[VIV...

A sexy administration.

Should I?   That's funny.

Better. A ghost story.
Talking to the dead.
Can I get away with
writing ghost stories?
Edith Wharton wrote
ghost stories.

More wine?

Out the window, an
ancient beard in a
magenta beret toddling
penguinistically along.

It's amazing the cheap stories and
they're all true. Trains that meet up or

Bush, Dick and Colon.

Old joke. Don't repeat.

I wonder what the
ordinary problems are.
Or are these the ordinary
problems?

Like my story, my statue.
Is that an ordinary
problem?

Finish us off.

Out the window, mad
dash, fast fearful lad.

[VIV...

don't. Letters that don't arrive. You know?

There's no future for us. There's no future for any of the three of us.

You don't

Where would anyone even live?

I'm as tacky as a porcelain angel on the side table of a portable home.

New York.

The real story of *Enemy of my Enemy*.

The real story of that part of *Enemy* was my birth grandmother, who wouldn't meet with me, not her way to meet with the presumptuous grandchildren who enter the world sinfully and were back stirring up trouble needlessly. This is all assumption on my part. I never met her. My sister Elizabeth told me the story about her, about Guinevere my grandmother, that she married a guy when she was young and divorced him and then had a bunch of kids with her second husband, including Shirley, and then he died, and then she remarried her first husband when

How drunk am I? 7.2? 6.7? Drunk enough. Drunk enough to forgive myself later.

Love buried and dug up again.

You can't

We must be very drunk.

New York.

Look how many
people in here now.
Families, lovers.
Didn't even notice.

[VIV...

The way my tongue swerves over these words, dekes and dribbles, like deep kisses.

she was, like, sixty-two, and they stayed together for, like, fourteen years after.

The love.

Love and time.

Take me home.

Time and love.

Take me wherever.

Life in a small town.

Tim's the statue buried
and dug up and stolen.

Are we drunk enough?

I should take her home.

Let's go.

Or wherever.

Cheque at my right hand
and like love like Tim I
didn't have to ask.

3

Life of Flesh

You've Been Promised Love

Fiddling with new currency, calculating an inappropriate tip, Clive stands up wondering where Viv's wandered to. Frozen behind aquarium glass, searching for her face in the middle of so much bubbletalk in so many languages he doesn't understand, Clive yearns until there she is. Outside. Standing on the corner outside, crossing and recrossing her legs like she's dancing.

You've Been Promised the Mess We're In

Viv is rehearsing ballerina steps from fifteen lives ago. First to second to third to fourth to fifth position. Again: closed open, closed open, closed. Again: they'll spend the night together naked one way or another. Clive strides out the door to the corner, slats the palm of his hand between her coat and the pitching roll of her spine. Her head on his shoulder. The selfish world's on the verge of collapse with nothing or next to nothing to be done about it.

If You Were a Stranger

She's wearing a black dress obviously more elaborate than what she usually hides herself in, that's clear. He's managed a roughly drab but clean collared shirt, a professional traveler's outfit. Possibly a journalist. You might guess that. Their unstylish bodies are a bit glam tonight despite ragged middle youthfulness, a bit intelligent the way they press against each other. But you probably wouldn't notice.

If You Were a Friend

A brooding tenderness closely related to confusion, guilt of betrayal linked with ferocious remnants of loyalty, a mishmash of desperate and civilized, lost and found, relieved and sorrowed, full and empty. There's fear and raw restraining exhaustion draped over them like scarves, like they're poor orphaned siblings clutching each other on the corner.

Aching for nakedness, and hungering to forget, and knowing it's a waste of time, and despising the waste of time, and imagining you must look like you're dead staring out at the metamorphosis, lusting for flux like the curious ghosts of children.

You've Been Promised A Night in Buenos Aires

The sky has congealed with nightscum. The city smells like skin. With the wind swirling, the fall confused with spring, the sparrows squabble back to their delayed scavenges. The rain has reined itself in. Above the corner buildings with the ground floors cut out from under them for obscure tax purposes rise the thousand thousand rooms of makeup and gossipy phone calls and curling irons and quickies before parties and gin fizzes and perfume spritzes in coy armpits and belly growls and air kisses.

The sick and tired taxi driver arrives, honking irritated Babel, to speed them through Palermo Viejo, through the night streets, through their silences, through and in between dinner and sleep.

There's always the other side of the world, half forgotten always. Driving through a city they don't understand, cannot understand, will never understand, their hidden crimes begging to be stripped from them.

They arrive dazed in the exposed concrete and gilt foyer of the apartment building without remembering how exactly. No recollection of the route or the fare or the slam of the car door.

The stand-up comedians in their stomachs suddenly don't find the prepped jokes funny anymore. A small, tough crowd. A small silent room rising to other rooms bumpy with jumpy mechanical jerks and rumbles and the blood flutters. When the door opens, a fluorescent hallway to fumble with keys.

You've Been Promised

Who have fumbled with keys before, who have returned before to rooms they don't remember, who have stumbled into fluorescent hallways, their lives banged around as merrily as pinballs into semi-paradises, into strangers' rooms, and who have learned how to step into the way of the people they love and out of the way of everybody else, who know enough to keep trying the keys until one fits.

Where do they hang their coats? What does it mean? What's hidden?
What's open? And who? And why? And what's the big deal? And
what's caged in their eyes? And what's pulsing? And who's there?

It's a wonderful
apartment, Clive.

The best I could find
in a week anyway.

Was it very
expensive?

It was cheap. And you
know what it means
when I say that.

Like, free.

Yeah.

I think I was supposed
to say something
about tomorrow.

They throw their coats on the arm of a sofa. Their clothed bodies are
hidden. A book about the art of Xul Solar is open on the side table.

What do you do?

You don't waste time.

You unhitch your dress straps from their clavicle hangers.

First right then left.

You let your covering slip away.

And you step out of it like it's a darkness puddle.

Then you snap your bra. The hook is at the front.

It springs away like night rind.

You let it fall apart like knifed fruit.

And you curl the edges of the stretch-lacies down and let them glide away.

And you stand there naked.

Looking in his eye.

You watch and wait.

You liken the width of her exposed shoulders to violas.

You want.

You watch as she lets her dress slip away.

And she steps out of it like a darkness puddle.

Near to you.

Her breasts like curving smoke.

Her stomach.

The rolled edges of the last garment reveal the fringes of truth then truth.

And you watch her naked.

Looking in her eye.

First Kiss

Their hands begin to skim their body leaves, skim all the half-hidden, half-revealed histories, run over all the surfaces, thumb the corners. Eyes limpid, darkling, they cannot see the lips roamed to their lips, breath smothering wine-stained breath, neither realize the cheek shut against cheek like folded fans, the crow's feet at their eyes narcissused, and the brush of eyebrow against eyebrow street-crossing like perfumes scuffling. They cannot see. They will not, won't, inspiring proximity, nakedness in all and many senses. It's no kind of statement to Clive and Viv, neither will nor testament, nor manifesto, nor manual of instruction. It's no statement of any kind at all. She rubs the top of her foot against the veiny, tendony flippers of his arches so variable in their flexibility, so weak when angled for fishish hugs.

(*And as they reemerge …*)

Viv
I don't want you to …

Clive
What?

Viv
No, I want you to

Clive
You want me to?

Viv
Yeah.

They have to begin again, like children scampered to the playground after supper, tree climbing their lives of fleshes, his hands capturing her breasts like a daguerreotype, and his mouth like April rain down the Japanese crane of her rope-coiled neck.

A Timthought shivers slowly between them.

Resignation. The chill-draped air. An apartment in Buenos Aires. Her palms rouse from the beef of his back, the hick-rounded shoulders on the boy, into the fine sheer of hair. Rakes that smooth it into spumes. And he smells like tangerine shampoo, acid beverage cleanliness.

And then remembering a roadside in Malaysia, the abandoned children, brown as spilled chocolate milk, who sold her thick cuts of pineapple, a shower of brightness in the haze of poverty and tropics. Twilight and dawn confuse. Spring springs while fall falls.

Sighing, lounging, arced her left leg around the small of his back. Rubbed and kissed, she knows her ragged margins loosening. Air into her lungs: ungrained smoke. Mouth on her hip: white watercolour ovals. Feels good.

Tasting the side of her belly, the cage, the last rib, the under, the giving, and then the South Pacific island of her hip: atoll. Now he knows. Now he knows. Now he knows that the unsunned expanse of skin under her underarm is ever so, ever so sticky, like rice paper in mist.

Kisses. Belly bacon. He tries to be a constellation hung under her navel but he fails. His hands try to be symmetrical toboggans down the whole of her leg, knee, ankle, heel. He wants to be the architect of Roman roads down the curves. He frails.

No: her quiet. *Maybe:* her fingertips cobwebbing the short hairs on his neck nape, toying with his delicate sensitives, his head in the spot where a pregnant bride might hold a sunflower. Yes: then her palms gliding over his shoulder, brushing away immature wonder, calm invitation to desire.

The press of his face like handwriting pushes up into the furrow of her breasts. She's like the utter flush of freshly warmed worn clothes: as full as a classroom of children declining French verbs out loud.

And when she turns, as if to block a wind
that isn't blowing; when she sits up, as if
to pillow his shaggy head with her lathed
lap; when she glides herself beside him, so
they're like two cleavers in the knife drawer,
she pushes him, squatted unconformingly,
down, down, down, down under and aside
her. So she can rise over him like pollution.

Her left hand hampers to the half-cool muscle of his back-
side, horseformed haunch, his penis stamping its feet, word-
shy labourer, on the porch.

Remembering the symmetry of seashells
while he smooths the spine between her
shoulder blades' vestigial angel wings, down,
down, down to the creases, the soft crescents.

Uncouth his thick cock flips up, underthigh to over-
belly, and they both laugh, drunklike. Blood pump.
Flashes of many possible futures. And her hand
reaches down to baton it for a reminiscence. And
she sits up quick, and she, and she leans over to lick.

This will just be brief. She kisses quick its tip, and she
licks around the crown, and kisses moistening the half,
like a demure sip, and the sound, like the salt tide in rust
pipes—glugged pleasure—mixes with the rustle of ma-
chines upstarting down airshafts, and the fury of some
driver on some street tonight somewhere.

Arms crossed behind his head, splayed farmboy on
haystack. In her warm mouth, circles, countercir-
cles, the hot spurt inside him rousing like dawn inside a gilded cathedral dome. Goodness.

And he tries to think, as he always tries to think in these situations of the essay the principal of his junior high school, Mr. MacGregor, of shaggy moustache and shaggier memory, would assign as punishment: ten pages describing the inside of a ping-pong ball. How to write it?

Half his penis down her mouth fit searchingly. The feel of the hard rib-like veins against her wet lips up and down. Underpump of the *corpora cavernosa* on the muscle of her tongue. The tender scrotum, the pubic scraggliness around her hooping palm.

She slouches in the furniture of her mind, watching her hand sculpting his clayey penis. The taste of that Malay pineapple. Bloody steak. The dieseled ride into the airport charred like wet leaves in her memory. Gross smoke. Is it languor? Is it a breather? Before?

Fed and forlorn: fed by the freshness of her grasp, forlorn by the freshness of oxygen.

Like sudden weather, with a quick end kiss, she unmouths it from her, lounging her head on his desert stone hip. She watches her fingers, her French-manicured nails, as she pulls and pulls the wet smooth red.

Viv
That was magnificent steak tonight.

Clive
The wine too.

Viv
Magnificent wine.

Clive
Magnificent.

Viv
And those sweetbreads ...

Clive gets an idea. It's not the most original idea but it's a good idea nevertheless. A magnificent idea even. Rappel down the proud hips with his manhandled grip. Finger. Tongue tip.

Not and not
There yet
Wet there, don't cry over spilt milk
And I remember this part of my body, yes, this is the amazing part
There
A water cup crowned with a single drop of oil
Concentrate
The rind of the pomegranate cracked like an aunt's laugh
Spilling seven seeds
Crushed against the mouth's roof there
There was a time
(the back of my head sunk into the pillow plush)
Toomuchtoomuchtoomuchtoomuch
Ouch,nothing,nada,niente,rien
Ouch
Start again

Tim is lying flat on his back on the other side of the world
Thinking about Clive eating me out
But eating me out is exactly the correct expression
There and there and there
There yes
And
My down
There?
Nothing, it vanishes gone

Moved too soon.
I should have fooled around longer.
Is this too soon? Should I go back?
Should I not collect two hundred dollars, not pass go?

The brink of a pool of woman.
Couldn't make Diane come this way. Too much?
Which is weird. It's too much.
Oops.
And therefore we slow and we slow and start again.
I don't make excuses. If Diane didn't come, I'm not saying she can't come.
I'm just saying that I'm not the guy who could make her come.
I gave my all.
Tim. Must not think.
A violation of all trust.

Whither loyalty?

And there go her legs her hips beautifully spreading gorgeous.
The brink.

That would have been too soon anyway
I forgot to call my mother yesterday for her birthday
Which mother?
Which me?
Relaxed like the spa or the caw of the raven with the branch in its maw
Or the flaw healing or just not mattering anymaw
Or the red green carpet softly tattering after the pattering of gorgeous feet
nattering
Good no matter what
Is it me when I come?
Or is it out there?
Say a desert all around or the snow field no sound
A figure approaching or am I approaching?
Encroaching
Space suddenly
There
Then out there
Then here then there
Maybe like stepping through a waterfall
And the waterfall's me
I must be trying too hard but it doesn't matter
Because the figure exclamation point
Is coming
There
And will be there
There
It's coming fast and faster
Suddenly there
and then there

It's funny.
This is what they call being good in bed.

The grand crescendo. The bolero.

Wonder when this started? Ancient Mesopotamia probably like my
statues like his statues like their statues I hope I get to see it tomorrow
or if not tomorrow how will he get it to New York?
I guess they know how to work that shit out.

Love her.

She tastes like pickled lemon, or no, no, the lemon stuffed
into the flanks of charred snapper.

Tang.

I wonder what it's like to eat actual cat.

Imagine all the oceans concentrated into a tear

Is it me or the lapping on the shore?

Him, him there

Or

Me, me there

Or

(Wait)

Is it

Me?

(where?)

There?

Is it

You know what would make a good euphemism? The word lexicography.

I've always thought that.

It's not that different from spreading a book and licking the spine.

I think they call that the gutter. The lexicographers.

I mean the bibliographers.

(Wait)

Is she?

She's going to.

I think.

Is she?

There

Sounding and astounding

Resounding and running and rousing

Slivering and silvering and spilling and slippering

Raining and running and rushing

Slumping and slouching

There

There she is
There she is

It seems we like to perform a trick on ourselves: spread
out our bodies like paper, scribble a word, erase it, forget.
It gives us the temporary illusion of having begun again.

Livid with
the sunshiny trumpet-
ing hip upthrust and blast,
he's licking the last glamour off
the half-shell, the last glimpse of
whatever revelation she may be en-
countering on the hilltop, truth
and nothingness, no, yes
until the end of
the end.

Viv's crumpled, foetal, curled away like
a wounded deer in a stand of alder.

Clive's already rustling in the bedside table drawer for the condom
carefully plotted there. The rip of a candy wrapper. The waft of
Nonoxynol-9 like an industrial site. He's rolling the equipment
down his shaft with all the precision of assassin or junkie, and she's
hungry to write the word again. Maybe this time she'll remember.

Put her below me because she's
eager turned toward me Viv open
who are we who buy ties and an-
swer the tele-
phone O I'm
hot or her
palm's cool
turning me
down stiff to
the gate O

Fitting, not quite, like an awkward
geometer's puzzle in pieces about
to fall into the elegant solution always prepared for it. Their brutish-
ness swells—ape sympathy, hawk
tenderness in stick nests, the muc-
kymuck, sweet-sticky pupae and
the delicate unfurling of helio-
trope ferns—as they begin to cast
their shadows into each another.

Take him
put him
there and
in again
and again
why do we do this why we
need this how must this feel
how must it gentle now gen-
tle and we must we must gentle

Into her and into her, millimeter after millimeter, the delicate embrasure, thick pleasure, the brown bird against the green field looks red as it glides over the blue river, and the rings of honey water become crowns of milky desire, become rose-glory arbors, while his stomach muscles flex, and he can't push too much or back at all, so she's waiting until the whole of his fierce muscle slides into her when she can gauge the thrust of his meaning, or the meaning of his thrust, whichever. Meanwhile poise. She utters **yes**, and he, having forgotten to breathe or swallow or how to breathe or swallow, remembers with coughed spit breath.

 His pubic arch prows into the knuckle of her clitoris

Cupid and Psyche, they could be any two

Chaereas and Callirhoe, Leucippe and Clitophon, Chloe and Daphnis

Can't stop now can't pause
can't stay this way endlessly
O I must swallow backwards

now and
I can't go
can't go
yes no

Nearly as slowly, like the gaze of
when will we meet again as the
train aches from the station, he
strokes himself out, delicious as a
summer swimmer hauling his sop-
ping body into the tropical night
air, and for another plunge, high
dive from the rocks overhead,
into the oblivious pond, the un-
sounded depths of the dark lake.

Nothing
nothing to
say noth-
ing to dis-
play noth-
ing to do play overtures to
the O throwing the bronze-
ball and moth against the
bell and stars

Now

All the statues in stone and bronze and gold

Are searching out intimate rooms in Buenos Aires to listen to Carlos Gardel

The public squares will be utterly bare

Slow and slow and slow and lengthen your stroke like the rowing team all in order with their tanned backs and the little coxswain which is the pubic bone to clitoris excellent nuzzle it just a little bit and the oar cuts the water without foam pulls without splash miniature maelstrom

The pace, of the brunt, isn't short, isn't long, isn't too short, isn't too long, their faces touch, cheek and ear and eye brushing ear and eye and cheek, and he slows down, under her shoulder he holds her, in the bookstand of his arms he holds her, under him, her knees rise, sodden and sunken her thighs rising open, the hip joints thudded, the hip joints thudded open, her knees and her arms circle his neck, his back, the middle of his back, the small of his neck, and her moaning lifts, his grunts like the beginning of hail.

I wonder if the condom's any good since he must have brought it with him from Arab-land and how good can the condoms be there but can South American condoms be any reliabler I mean more reliable

Second Kiss

Looking into each another, as if by chance, their eyes shut like shutters thrown open into a morning courtyard, lips clutched, thoughtless in the smell of squeeze, the overproof booze of the submission to forgetfulness which has a kind of funny aftertaste like overripe blueberries and pencil shavings, their cores rubbed down by terry cloths, all at the pace of a parade waving high yellow flags and circling in their own circles with the calm stasis of undermusic heard, if heard at all, as a kind of thorougher, or more thorough, silence.

The garbled chum of the slaughter siphons into scum sewers

Life of flesh

Pans collect the crush of apples and olives dewed under screw presses

Light-dappled tabletop and paper where the word is about to be written

Which you read without understanding

And then forget

And now, over the lawns and in the gardens of the grand estate

The children are running to secret places

Playing hiding and seek

Evening is falling

Where are you?

Into which delicious corner have you tucked your little gorgeousness?

The time has come Clive to start
considering the things which are
complicated so please explain to
us Clive exactly how you would de-
scribe the inside And no longer does the rhythm
of a ping-pong of his thrust, though it synco-
ball and you pates with her dark **hehs**, his light
have ten pages **hahs**, the drugged splurge of ani-
so please begin mal rightness inside them, no lon-
immediately ger does it glide along surfaces; no,   *I want to be on*
out in the hall it squats in their guts, an aquar-   *top I'm sure the*
ium water while the fish flop and   *condom is fine*
surmount, an elevator rising to   *but I want to*
the top of a building with no top.   *be on top his*
                                       good heart's
                 pumping through my veins but I
                 want to be on top he's finely slowing
                 but I want to be on top the night
                 is running with death but I want

180

Pause. The sheen of his long frog muscle boasts in her, insisting politely on its pulse. The lovers roll aside, stroke, stroke each other's arms as if they had the wings of swans, stare, stare into each other's eyes. And she adjusts, around her hips, around him, rousing a dazed flutter of minor craving. A decision must be made about how to distribute these ecstasies.

Viv
Hi.

Clive
Hello.

Viv
I'm just going to ...

Clive
Sure.

Viv
Let me just. OK. Let me ...

Clive
Like? Oops.

She takes him in her hand—the latexed shaft smothered and smoothed with her ferment—and she holds him, under her, to the edges, and when he's tucked, slides herself down until they both gentle, even her breasts relaxing as she slides down, and down to drown him with the full array of her hair, and at last settles on him like a stop-motion sunset, purples into reds, browns, greens and blacks, like chromatic chords, like the smell of browned apple and lemon sugar, and come to a rest when she's over all of him.

Buenos Aires

Night has fallen and the children haven't returned

The bright wet crisp summer morning has gathered night storms now

Where are you?

The house is empty and the gardens are bare

The storm gathering

And the children aren't anywhere

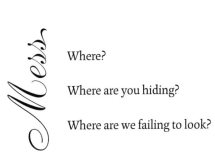 Where?

Where are you hiding?

Where are we failing to look?

Children see lightning flashes and understand instantly

The world beyond is illuminated and destroyed in the moment of illumination

And the question is whether to start crying or run out into it

I'm not going to slow make him come
no he won't yes he will and some
long time ago couldn't with a new
me hope that condom works wher-

ever he bought
it and Clive
is a beauti-
ful and strong
and good man

She rises down, her hair collaps-
ing up, and she rises again like
an avalanche, falling like a crash
of sparks, raising ruins that crumble into architecture, and she
leaps up into the abysses sink-
ing into empyreum, and soars
into the underworld plum-
meting through seven circles.

Yes no she's
a flagrant
woman yes a
woman alive
in the life of
flesh and her

hair tossed like a woman tosses
her hair in joy dancing in the
dust reveling in the joy yes no

187

He smells rough with the city lust
he must have come off the des-
ert in the glare of background
blue tough funny that this is how
life goes on
or a reason-
able facsim-
ile thereof the
supreme joke

This is the only Throne. This is the only Throne of Bue-nos and this is the only Throne of Aires. This is the only Throne of Love. This is the only Throne of the Mess We're In. This is the only Throne of the No and the only Throne of the Yes.

Waverings and bounces, guts trem-
oring, with or without knowing
what they're doing. Their hands
are clenching, and clenched hands
cannot become one hand, and
clenched hands cannot tell hand
from hand, and the improvised
fist—hints, reflections of reflections, suggestions of suggestions,
detective raids into the half-dark.

Her breast
her breasts
I don't care
the curves
let me shel-
ter her other

soft tenders the slopes cut the
cut slopes crescents and the tus-
sle a rough dog with a bit of gris-
tle in its maw whistle whistle

Flagrantly I don't care Clive returned
from Jordan that week with desert sand
in his shoe poured it into the lake hug-
ging Tim I
don't want to
know I want
to the smile
of his lips
on the dock
I don't care
I want to

Time to
make a
decision
a b o u t
whether
y o u ' r e
g o i n g
to wait
no sur-
prise we

have no time she has and she knows shat-
tered windows hammer and tongs round
gongs rung roundly all my many wrongs longs

And here I can see he's standing at the
door his strong face at the door with
that smile he wore yes through me his
hands are
where there
found you
found you
found there

Time to
yes time
to give
yes time
to release
into her
atmosphere the seed up on her
the hips shelf breasts bound
lovely contortion of her soft face

Triumphing into a migraine or
the glorious procession under
the bannered arches of the city of
cities will she
crash or float
through all
matter like?

Behind him
beyond him
a root uptug-
ging rugged
unplugged
soggy with
dirty tendrils crumbly earth-
guts shaking off into daylight
a rich scruff of soil coming

 The children's faces raptured by the lightning flashes

 Blood-soaked Carlos Gardel laughs with an arm crooked
round the neck of a gypsy statue

No

Yes

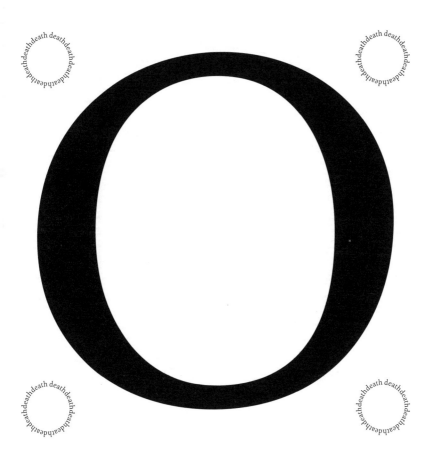

Nothing, no one, night, blackness, dark, the inside of the ping-pong ball, everclosed box, unknown and unknowable, zero, cipher, empty space beyond space, forgetfulness, blank, blot, void, interiors of men and women, oblivion, the end.

what is this what is this what is this what is this what is this what is this what is this what is this what is this what is this what is this what is this what is this what is this what is this what is this what is this what is this what is this what is this

Sound-
ing & astounding re-
sounding & running & rous-
ing slivering & silvering & spilling
& slippering raining & running & rushing slumping & slouching sounding & astounding resounding & running & rousing slivering & silvering & spilling & slippering raining
& running & rushing slumping & slouching sounding & astounding resounding & running & rousing
slivering & silvering & spilling & slippering raining
& running & rushing slumping & slouching sounding & astounding resounding & running & rousing
slivering & silvering & spilling & slippering raining & running & rushing slumping & slouching sounding & astounding resounding &
running & rousing slivering & silvering
& spilling & slippering raining &
running & rushing slumping
& & & & & & & &

Bathing in the world overstarted. Theme of degeneration and regeneration. How life begins again.

Raised
from the shudder,
lost in the mutual of after
lost consciousness, their skins
surface into each other, salt glints
of darkness, seeping into glimpses
of their sweat and transience, like
whale bones dredged from sea
dust, settled into a kind of sur-
prised togetherness, their
bodies halfhealed half-
defeated.

The pines are restless. The red blanket of rusted needles and the sound of soughing resist the rush of distant waters, the hewed flakes of the crackling bark, the pungent and insistent smell of the sap in the pines far far away.

4

Seventeen Constellations
& A Map of New York

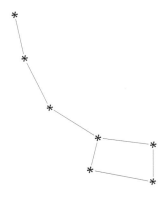

Never try to describe people's dreams. Leave dreamers alone. Leave them on the balcony, on unsteady plastic chairs beside geranium pots with the lights off, in cotton robes which are far too thin for the blustery gusts tumbling through the clusters of buildings, the avian labyrinths of highrises constructed accidentally for the amusements of pigeons.

"A glass of water?" he asks.

"Nothing," she replies.

Below them swells the constellationry of a city, the gasoline smell of the judgments of others, the mild roar of the indistinct somewhere. Leave them to the darkness and the stars.

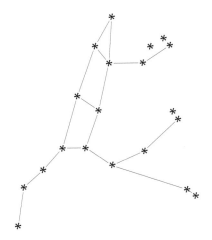

On the other side of the world, in another bed, Tim cannot locate by sonar, drilling, luck or persistence, a precious vein of unconsciousness in the rock darkness of his mind. No amount of square breathing, it seems, can plaster his cracks, neither counting in series backwards, backwards by evens, backwards by sevens. Tim lies in wait for sleep. In the night's belly, Tim likes to read his bedside atlas by the light of the moon. The book of the world opens with a creak. Insomnia umbrellas. His finger flutters to central Asia, traces a soft journey across the surfaces, a freedom out of the unimpeded and ideal conception of Polo or Battuta.

"I will never ..." he's whispering so Annie, the night guard, won't hear.

The moon drags its tired ass up, weary to death with its allusiveness, boring itself in the sky. Reflection is spreading mayonnaise over the back lawn of the care centre, the Apriled and now Mayed lawn glitter-chiming with dew, vulgarized by the malapropism of a half-dozen Adirondack chairs where lithium groups tend to settle during the nothingness of the afternoons, afternoons measured by the tosses of tennis balls to

Labrador retrievers, afternoons measured by boxes of Ritz crack-
ers. Tim's midnights—this is not the first—are antidotes to such
afternoons.

"Best not disturb Annie."

From the underside of his mattress a solitary dime, a coin
lunar in its delicacy, stamped with a Queen's face. A Canadian
dime glimmering in the moonlight is one of the most beautiful
objects the earth has ever produced: the reflection of a reflection of a reflection.

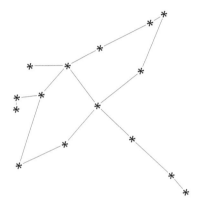

Guard Annie sits at her terminal watching *Die Hard 2* on the
smallest of eighteen screens, polishing a Spartan apple on her
thigh, shifting haunch to haunch to haunch on the just-broken-
enough-not-to-fix chair and flirting with the idea of a phone
call to her son Justin in North Carolina. He would still be up
most likely, either with his books—always an excellent student,
93 percent out of high school—or with his men friends, doing
whatever it is they do. On screen a plane crashes, crushing the
ground. Nothing you can do to a Spartan will scrape the waxi-
ness off that first crunch and Justin wouldn't answer at this hour
anyway.

With practiced rat fingers Tim works the dime through the gristly grate on his window. Edging through, he gives the coin a screwdriver's implication. Unloosening the bolts one by one, corner by corner, southeast, northeast, northwest, southwest.

The grate dissevers. Openness.

"Delightful. No other term. I must leap. It must be Spring. Leap down into it. The loveliness, yes, yes, the gift of a Spring night."

How barefoot he is, squelching across the dewy lawn which has turned confetti-white not under the influence of the encyclical moon but under the everlasting thrum of the asylum lights beaming equally over the ground even to the corners where no one might contemplate traipsing. Tim's wearing very little, a ragged Club Monaco T-shirt and lilac pajama bottoms floraled with purpleish roses, yet it's impossible to distinguish whether the shiver syncopating his stride draws its jerk and rhythm from cold or pleasure. He's heading beyond the wall.

The magnificent oak tree looms from the edge like a skeletal ice cream cone, like graveyard freedom.

Sprinting to the wall, jacking up like skin-the-cat, he manages to catch a dipping branch, manages, commandorifically, to hoist himself, shimmying, up and across.

On the other side of the wall, darkness. Beyond the asylumic fluorescence, the semi-wild loneliness of the moon gone solo again with the seven stars for backup singers. Under still anatomies of bare maples, Tim is insane. His soul is flammable and the spring is showering sparks over him while he waits—waits for what?— waits for his rods and cones to swivel and roll among the new-started beauties upslouching in budges within the hedge bindweed, yarrow and bethorned evening primrose, waits for the not-yet-bud from under the stank rot of the maple leaf blanket and bracken. Tim creeps like a golem to a rock furzed with dank lovely ground moss, squatting, reconnoitering.

"Beyond the grate was the window and beyond the window was the lawn. Was the lawn. Beyond the lawn, a wall. A wall into midnight. Beyond midnight runs the river."

Into the silence a terrific lack of animal motion enters. Not a porcupine, not a muskrat, not a vole so much as turns to its side. And yet. Like a woodcock huddled under the leaves with her chicks ready to flush, fear looks like it's about to call him up, or not, depending on where he sets his next step.

"Yes and no. Before all that. All that I did. All that I have done. *Bucephala islandica. Bucephala islandica.*"

Never before has he stolen barefoot among such barbed twigs, the hurtful sabotages underfoot, through such deliciousness of revitalization—but not his revitalization—such clashes of miracles weaving and wefting the dead stuff of winter with rot's handicraftsmanship. Tim's a natural historian, remember. Known by its rough names, he recalls, rot is shaggy mane, giant puffball, elegant stinkhorn, destroying angel, wolf's milk slime. Tim's mind is like the forest floor constelled with a million million branches of pain and lurking spores.

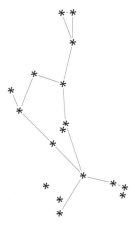

And so Luna and her lunatic catch through the notorious scrim of semi-wilderness the first flicker of the flow of the river. (Well, call it a creek.) Its flow washes away the sediment of many evil thoughts, and the sound of its flow is a soothe.

"Beyond. Before and beyond."

Down to the creek. (Call it a stream.)

"And never to…"

On cracked feet, soles ripped by broken half-frozen branches and the sharp stones of the degenerate world, no owl careened into his foolishness. The lilac pajamas couldn't cover this caper. Crazy. In the dark, dark, dark. He wades to and into and through the chilling watercourse.

"I will have to genuflect. The ice palace. The stone cavern. The cave. The cave. Before and beyond. Beyond. Before. Where?"

In the river or the creek or whatever, Tim sees dilapidated time's riot. So cold. His insanity knows—Tim doesn't yet—that he's not going back from the river, through the woods, over the wall, across the lawn, into the window, into his bed, under the covers. No. The cold is like a cavity he's crawled into.

"And he said you can never step into the same river once. Right. Right. Before and beyond. Before and beyond. Beyond, beyond, beyond."

Tim sits on a rock in the middle. On this rock, he unbuilds himself.

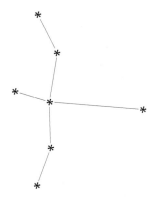

Toes cramp stoneside. His forehead touches his kneecaps. Death peers from the darkness. He's laughing and sobbing, in flames. Why? What?

Either many many long moments pass or brief eternity.

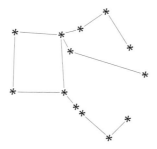

Either the burgeoning of the world, turtleheaded before its ever-fresh routine, the unleashing of dandelion and buttercup, crop of Queen Anne's lace, snow trillium, cinquefoil stomped by badger and skunk, thickened like soup by dogwood and sedgegrass, mimics his own deluge of soul as yet untuned, disreasoned, or he falls into time like a child into the undertow. Into the dark, dark, dark. A sharp stone from the cold water. He's crazy. He's in the dark. He knows.

The moon dips and the stars disaster and Tim gashes into his wrist, sucking the remnants on the embers. Why? Why? Ribbons of black red. Bleeding into the stream. (Or the creek or whatever.)

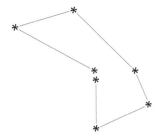

The nightrambling waters of the north slick him as he falls, and in the aches of rushing cold, madness ebbs from him into a new darkness without things.

In the morning, a police dog named Finnegan will smell Tim out, Annie's going to be fired, the appropriate authorities will decide, after consideration, to remove the tree branch overhanging the wall, and together Clive and Viv will fly back for the funeral, trading autumn for spring, and Clive will abandon his story for *The Atlantic* about Iraqi art theft, and it will turn out that Viv is pregnant, and she and Clive will talk it over and decided that they have to keep it, because life is better than death, and they will decide that they have to move to New York, because it's the only place, and so they will wait for the baby, and she'll come, a little baby girl named Chloe like a red bird descending into a used car lot, and three months later the new family will cab to the airport and race like a stress clot down the tunnel past the gate toward the rest of the world, and that's how they'll end up in New York, with a baby and everything.

5

Morning in Brooklyn

Quiet

Friday night turns into Saturday morning even along Fourth Avenue in Brooklyn. Six lanes all hours all night have rumbled in and out and stalled and passed the river of coming and going while regular round red-lit emergencies red-seaed the traffic with ancient wailing fury and alarm—a few youngish Park-Slopers glanced at the commotion over their shoulders sluicing into and out of the subway from Manhattan posing adventures—and Clive and Viv and Chloe, in their sixth floor apartment mistily infused with the racket, slept, sort of.

Interruptions

Viv has nursed Chloe four times over the course of the night: before bed at 6:37, at 10:09, again at 11:13, and then again around 4:30. Each time the baby cries she stumbles up like an electroshocked drunk, dragging her loaded iPod through the dark into Chloe's chamber. The iPod helps. The larger world's accumulated chatter—inner city little leagues, Guantanamo torture, the collapse of a piece of ice the size of Cleveland off the polar shelf—amounts to a kind of comfort.

Whenever Viv rises, Clive half-rises, listens cocked out of half-sleep while his wife's succouring arms bring silence. Twenty minutes later the dreaded transfer to the crib begins, when the baby's renewed wails start the whole process over again, or quiet followed by clicked relief as the side of the crib slats up.

Pieces

Their nights are broken like a broken chair or a broken leg, like the streetlight auras beginning to break the edges of their cheap plastic blinds (only Chloe has a blanket hung over her window to keep dark dark). Viv has not slept longer than a five-hour stretch for eleven months now. She's exhausted before she's up. Waking means no further hope of rest. Leaving bed means longing for bed. The light before morning grows desperately.

Cry

Where?Where?
Where?Where?
Alonealonealo
neWhereamI
IIIIIIIIIIII?

Heard

No. How can? Chloe? Are you? Miserable outrage of a what's wrong Chloe? Why won't that little girl sleep? My misfortune. Why can't her little body sleep longer than, like, forty-five minutes at a time? Maybe, maybe she'll fall back asleep. Remember that one time, like a week ago, she went down and back up again until 7:30. Maybe. Please O please O please O please. And I was in there like ten minutes ago. Please Chloe please.

Just like five more minutes, just five. Five. More. Five more minutes. Poor Viv, I wonder how last night with the numbness and the endlessness of all this. Desperate unbearable Viv. I wonder if Chloe. Like that one time. One time. Saturday morning means shopping for fish. Scrod. Like that one time, for five more minutes.

5:45

Sleep? Will you please fall asleep again Chloe? Please let her go to sleep again. I cannot go again. Why won't she sleep? Her bad luck to have such a bad mother. How can this? Why can't I get my baby to sleep? The question. Don't know anymore. But what am I supposed to do? Can't go back in there right? What time is it now? Time to liberate?

Alonealonealonealonealone whereareyouououououououououou?

Chloe is now up. I wonder what happened. Should leave her. If a baby cries in the forest. Disturbances? What disturbances? But seriously I think early, and then a bit in the middle, and then a bit, or two bits, at the end. Or something. Too early for me to take her, right? Night is the time you're supposed to be left without your parents.

Familiarity

I think she's up.

Yeah.

Do you want? Do you want to feed her? Or...?

I fed her like forty-five minutes ago

IIIIIIIIIIII
IIIIIIIIIIII
You ouououououo
uouououououo
uouououououo

I'll just take her to the market then and you can sleep a bit.

Wait. Isn't it too cold?

It's May.

I worry that it's too cold.

If it's too cold, I'll just take her for a short walk, and we'll come right back. I'll put on her hoodie.

Just go and get her.
I can't stand it.

How was last night?

The Arrangement

Viv and Clive have agreed to send Chloe to daycare so that Viv can write while Clive freelances but they have yet to find the perfect place in the neighbourhood with a spot and though Clive wants to travel more they moved to New York for his sake so they don't and Clive does most of the cooking but Viv is up in the middle of the night for Chloe because she has breasts and Clive takes her in the morning because he has the energy and on Saturday morning Clive takes Chloe to the farmer's market at Grand Army Plaza.

The Chambers

Clive scoops his pants off the floor and draws them over his tired ass quickly, quietly, while Viv flusters her head under the pillow so she doesn't have to listen to him heading down the hall to the room where Chloe is howling. It is well known that the torturers at Guantanamo Bay pipe the sound of babies crying into the rooms of their victims. Our biology is designed to be agonized by their helplessness.

First Hug

Chloe wakes up in a bare room, poor thing, all we put in was the bookshelf. And hung the socialist monkey print and the baseball fandango. Dangled the string of elephant figurines from India. She wakes up in, like, an artist's studio with nothing on the walls. Other mothers paint clouds all over the walls. They call that nesting. I'm a bare room. Is it more mother-guilt? I want to spend all my time with her but I can't stand to spend any more time with her. Next week a daycare no matter what.

Thanklove warmthflesh huggywarmth fleshthankyou andIandyouI

Good morning, sweetie. How are you ladybug, baby cocinelle? Listen, you've got to learn to sleep. Did you kill your poor mother last night, sweetie? Huh, smoocher? OK, more hugs, and then we're going to go to the market. We're going to get out of here right away so that mommy gets a whiff of sleep. First we're going to go into the hallway and then the living room and then the market. That OK? It's going to be so bright! So, so bright!

Surprises

Motherhood was supposed to be a revelation to Viv, or at least an accomplishment, a grant of security. Instead it's like a forest burnt to make space for the sky, for a love as vast as the sky.

Clive adores being a father. He loves handing Chloe's little body into his mother's arms. His brothers adore her delicacy too. They fight over who holds her and who plays with her. To them, even though Clive lives in New York on his wife's money, basically as a gigolo, he's all right. He's Chloe's father. He brought a girl into the family.

Life of Work and Flesh

The worst of Chloe's constant awakening and reawakening for Viv is that she can never write. She's never capable and she's already signed a contract for a novel about an 82-year old woman who has an affair with a 28-year old man, and all she has so far is the description of the woman's exhaustion, her vast exhaustion. And the title: *Oceans of Time*.

Clive carries his daughter into the living room and stands her at the coffee table so he can unbutton her sleeper (which he bought because of its ladybug pattern) and peels down her diaper (heavy with urine), wipes her labia nice and clean (and remembers the third, or maybe fourth, time he and Viv made love after Chloe's birth when a sudden letdown left his entire torso streaming with rivulets of breast milk). Chloe's first poo, he remembers, smeared out as thick and black as warm tar, and for a while, she peed pink; all, so they were informed, perfectly normal, recasting, instantly, the meaning of the term. And in the onrush of her mother's hormones after the birth Chloe's little baby breasts had spouted clotted tears of milk a little bit.

Hasty Outfit

Will she be warm enough now? That one time in April. Remember. He brought her back from Saturday, hands like ice. Hear him talking. He loves her. He'll have to put her in her thick jacket definitely. But then. Well. It is May. She might get too hot. Fifty degrees is like what Celsius? Forget it. Will he please check the weather before he goes. Layers are the key. No. Right, the hoodie.

Cloethesclotheschloechl otesupthearmupthe armdownthelegdown thelegdowntheleg throughthroughthrough chloetheschlotheschloec hlotheschloechloeclothe

Ladybug, ladybug, ladybug. And we put your arm in the arm, and we put your other arm through the other arm, and I'll get coffee outside, won't I? Good girl. And one leg up. And the other leg up, and we pull your pants right up to your waist, don't we? Yes! And daddy did bring the socks, yes, and we put one wee cutie into this patoottie. And another cutie into the other patootie, and I'm going to put on your hoodie, don't be moody, which I know you just love so much, and then your winter jacket just 'cause it's so, so early, and let's go tell your mother you're wearing layers. Yeah? Yeah!

Hasty Words

So we're going to go.

Did you put on ...

I put on her hoodie and her winter jacket and then if she gets hot I'll just take one off.

Thanks, lover.

Sleep.

I love you.

I love you too.

Escapes

Viv is already smoldering into that sleep of emptiness, an apartment without man or child, uninterruptible, the sweetest pomegranate darkness sleep, best of the week, real sleep. She slouches over her pillow, pulling herself over its softness toward whatever small comfort oblivion can bring while our bodies inflict themselves on us.

Out, out, out of the house. Quick. Out of its permanent unrest, its fume of latent exhaustion. Out of its love and boredom abysses. Clive looks at Chloe and Chloe looks at Clive. They understand despite scrunched, just-woken-up faces. Out. Hoodie on. Jacket on. Into the stroller. Check wallet. Check cell. Check keys. Out. Out now. Out into the Spring. Out into the world.

Morning Crossings

And when they're gone, and Viv's alone, she's so tired she needs to wait for sleep. She needs to wait for what she's waited for so long because she's waited so long for it. Dawn is the new evening in the confused twilight of her life.

Light or something like light. Too early I guess you call it a penumbra over the roofs of the houses across the street and no need for shade. Chloe hates shade. She hates (O a dead bird) a dead thrush of some kind. Right sidewalk there. (Life lesson for little girls.) No flies but maybe it's too early for the flies. Slow down a bit so I cannot help but stare into its dead eye. (God, I'm tired, little dead bird, I'm tired, I'm tired.) Nature's price for electric illuminated glory all its sky-reaching days, right? *And up we go, up we go, up we go, up. This is why they call it a slope sweetie.* To the market.

And so Clive and Chloe push up past ruinific Fifth Avenue, its width gorgeously deserted in the earliness of the hour, leaving Viv to jaywalk lazily across the last avenue of herself before oblivion.

Viv is falling asleep, although the precision of this common English phrase is dubious. It implies that sleep is a dark hole into which one falls, a zero, an 0 against which the 1 of daily life stands up. (And who is to say that the forms of our ciphers did not emerge from the abyss of the sleeper against the straight upstander?) The idea of sleep as opposed to wakefulness is the fundamental false binarism: light and dark, day and night, me and you, being and nothing. In truth, no line could be more blurred than the line between dreaming and daily living. The distant train whistle, overheard in the night, converts fluidly into a dreamt kettle boiling. How many times by day do we seem to recognize a dime caught in sunlight, a pitcher pouring milk, a book flashed open by the wind from that most selfish, most secretive of iconographies? Let's say Viv falls asleep insofar as she falls into the silence of the apartment without Clive and Chloe, a silence so much more than the mere absence of sound, the silence of sure solitude, the silence of her own.

And into that silence

Tim

O Tim, Tim, Tim, Tim, Tim

Tim

Clive and Viv share Tim like a crime they committed together. Love is no kind of bond compared to shame. Shame endures. Shame is patient. Their lives as parents, as partners, shiver always as a shared alias. They know each other as spies and traitors, with secret identities and clever disguises only the other can see through.

Chloe will never know Tim. This permanent lack, this happy and unhappy fate, increases the refreshing innocence of the little girl to her parents. She, at least, played absolutely no role, however minor, in their sordid trauerspiel.

Viv's several and discreet failures fuse like overlapped screens in her exhausted brain. Her inability to make her daughter sleep through the night mingles with her inability to assuage her dead mad husband's soul. She can fix neither the future nor the past. She is useless for all time.

And when she sleeps, she descends in dreams under the angled gold on the boughs of a rustling Northern forest, restless shadows under coolish shimmer of the light beside Lake Whiskyjack. It's the light from the busted shades they never bothered to fix.

Viv Descending

Clive needs bright spring apples, fresh. Clive needs fish, whitefish from the man with the boat. Tomatoes, tarragon. Spinach or equivalent. Clive needs eggs from the lovely Southern lady. Fish, eggs, tomatoes, greens, tarragon, a sweet. In the open-air marketplace under the muted gaze of the armies of the Republic, like a slow storm frozen on top of the wedding cake's arch.

The cottage stands where it stood. The tattered carpet, unpatterned puce, reveals frayed floorboards and a mound of tackle boxes, lacrosse sticks, a VCR, junk-crowded corners reveling in the inconsolabeauty of obsomnolescence. The most comfortable and most decrepit sofa in the world squats; the ordinance map of the lake on the plywood half-wall; the nineteenth century etching of a Summer Tanager—late menstrual blood red.

Tim is sitting at the card table in the kitchen, unshaven, back hunched over a plate of bacon and a chilled bowl of Cheerlessnessios.

Tim

You know what was the best thing about how we met? No music. Not so much as a radio.

Viv

I remember. I remember I would get in the car after a week in his middle of nowhere and listen to the eighties station all the way into town.

Tim

My car had a radio with no reception. And I was always a quiet lad. So why am I talking now, Viv?

Time wipes his lips gobsmackingly lumberjacklike on a flannel sleeve and swallows his mouthful of bacon.

When his crooked, fantastic, full lips open, his words fluster like poltergeist leaves across a canyoned street.

Tim

I wish you were dead. So you knew.

Viv

I'm so, so sorry.

Tim

No, just so you would know. You have every right to move on with your life. It's so easy to say I'll love you forever. But I'll love you this coming Wednesday at 8:15 in the evening? That's not so easy.

Viv

You stole that from W.H. Auden. I read that last night. Or was it this morning?

The boy's face like a leper prince's. His eyes are like blue milk, like moving juniper berries through fog.

Viv

The thing is, I'm comfortable with people who are that
dead. I started reading Auden because he recently turned
one hundred. In death years.

Tim

How nice for him. And for you. Why am I here?

Viv

I don't know why you're here.

Tim

O.

The stillness of the reflected pines on the waters of the lake outside the window belies the rushing counterfluster of air through the needlely branches.

Viv

You know, I wondered when you would come. And where. I've wanted to talk for so long. I thought it might be a grade-school classroom. I thought it might be a bookstore or a library. When I first saw Prospect Park, I thought, here. If only everyone would leave, he would appear. I'll go person to person asking them all to leave.

Tim

I love this lake. I do love it. Which must be why we're here. Look, my ducks, my ducks, Viv, look ...

She looks. The lake outside is bare, a black-blue shell. Three ducks descend, plashing the surfaces, breaking the moment apart.

Viv half-wakes into the half-light of her half-apartment in half-New York and kicks the half-puffed half of the duvet off her half-leg onto the floor where it half-settles like half an oyster on the half-shell.

Viv Ascending

Panic now always accompanies the moment of her waking, because when will she sleep if not now and she knows that sleeplessness sucks hope, alleviates the savour of the life of the flesh, tortures poor mommy, and her panic about sleeplessness can bring on sleeplessness, panic can engender the condition of her panic, but this morning her exhaustion trumps her panic about her exhaustion, and she goes back down easy, easy, easy.

She can almost see them in among the dogs of the Union Square market. "Yes sweetie, O she's a sweetie isn't she." "What's her name?" "He's Shady." "Yes, do you like her Chloe? Yeah? This is a corgi. This is the kind of dog Queen Elizabeth likes a lot." To the white suitleg: "She loves dogs." "She's such a sweet baby." To the perked, conic ears: "Bye Shady. Can you say bye-bye Chloe? Bye Shady." Father and daughter press on. There have been civilizations without fire without wheels without horses but no civilization without dogs.

One of the more interesting aspects of the natural history of Brooklyn is the existence of a small flock of parakeets in the borough. All explanations for their presence are necessarily speculative, but most ornithologists assume that the birds are pet refugees, perhaps accidentally released from Kennedy or La Guardia. The animals have survived for long enough that they must have bred in the city somewhere, somehow. Just like Clive and Viv.

Unknown Unknowns

And if they were to run into each other again, Clive, Viv, and Tim even after the adultery and the suicide and the betrayal, if they were once again to meet, not in some celestial columbarium but in a boozy dive, they would all sit and chat without reserve or hatred or even confusion. They would all understand one another. So the living think.

Humanity has developed a habit of uncovering more and more species as we extinguish them. We catalogue gigantic rats in Borneo volcanoes, newts in Guatemalan flowers, strange patchwork deer in valleys in the Andes, while the tiger vanishes. There's the famous case of the lighthouse keeper on a small South Pacific island, whose companionable cat kept bringing him offerings of dead birds, of a kind he could not recognize. The man sent a sample to the Royal Society in London, and they confirmed that the bird was indeed a new species, but by that time the cat had killed every last one.

The illumination of dawn or evening hasn't dimmed—
it's brightened backwards. The gilded wilderness reflects
a higher cosmic searching. Our marrow memories are
in these scenes of birds among trees among moss among
water: perpetual hidden insect orgies, quick unrecorded
genocides, the swelling of the twisted cloud pines over
eons, underearth fungus confirming the dead. The air
smells of shade, of broken light.

Viv

I love you more than I'll ever love Clive. With you I remember thinking, Give me everything. I want to be at the
bottom of things.

Tim

I don't know to womb one makes these requests but I
can't help you. I'm nuts.

Viv

You're macadamian.

Tim

A guy walks into a bar and the nuts say to him, 'your hair
looks nice today.' The guy asks the bartender, 'what's up
with the nuts?' And the bartender says, 'O, the nuts are
complimentary.'

Viv

Do you think it would be different if we'd had children?

Tim

Having a child seems to be driving you mad. Why would a child save me from madness?

Viv

The dollop of hope. She might be enough hope to form a shadow for you to hide under.

Tim

If only we could hide in our own shadows. That's an excellent definition of madness. Hiding in our own shadows. Excellent.

Viv

Let me tell you about Clive and Chloe.

Tim

Don't bother. I don't care. Like everybody else, they will get about as much time as the crushed skull of the abortion gets from the vacuum cleaner to the garbage can. We see about that much light. The cheapness of life is incredible. The only thing worth less is everything else. There should be no 'he' or 'she.' Just it, it, it, it.

She can sense his imminent departure like a long-clenched fist inside her, a fist clenched so long and so hard that she will soon have to let go, and the blood will rush back through her releasing.

Viv

I'm still happy you're with me. I'm happy to have you here.

Tim

Why?

Viv

A place apart. Not the news. Not a white courtyard, kids in fatigues with machine guns, robed men, veiled women, scared children, stumbling, being pushed around, not artistic mass murders, not blown-up Buddhas, new drugs, lost species, stolen alabaster statuettes of love goddesses. I still have love in the middle of the mess we're in.

Tim

Love is the mess we're in, Viv. Look, look ...

They look out, Tim and Viv, together, look out at the straggling survivors of an almost extinguished species of elaborate duck gliding across the surface of the lake and everything. Gunshot. Everything scatters.

And Tim scatters

the world and Tim and Clive and Chloe and Viv slips into the dark that swallows time and

249

Homecoming

Later, when Viv wakes, when she's rested or a reasonable facsimile thereof, she misses Clive and Chloe, and mercifully cannot remember anything. She wants whatever's in the kitchen.

Wait. See. I'll wait and see. Still. I'm as tired as a double-shift ender. It is inconceivable to me that people spend mornings in a church or in a synagogue or in a mosque. Beyond comprehension with the light streaming down, teasing down, careening down like this off the window-eyeballed buildings, the tambourine-leaved trees. And into pink bird foetus it looks like. Or something. Something dead.

Both Clive and Viv are crossing back to each other, across sleep, across Brooklyn. Biology is a boat for navigating rough currents.

Bedroom and Street

The stagnancy of sleeplessness, like the air has been breathed too much, grays the walls and flattens the tossingbody-tossed sheets and a couple of night-bubbled water glasses, some spine-cracking-splayed books on an Ikea bedside table and a pile of shelter magazines on the floor beside dust and wires, detritus of forgotten functions. Viv scratches her tired hair for the window's benefit and before she raises the blind, the confectionery music-box jingle of an ice-cream truck on the corner.

The street's an overturned bird-pecked garbage bag leaking rot-sodden rice and beans smeared over sushi packaging and a creamy black doll around which Clive wheels the stroller over the candy crackle of smashed sherry bottle shards to the front door. He hears the confectionery music-box jingle of an ice-cream truck on the corner.

Home and Away

She wants to write it all down. She wants *Oceans of Time* to be, to become, and the hope of its becoming lifts her from the bed to the floor. There will have to be breakfast first. The story of a woman who cannot forgive herself, who wants to live again, who wants night in a new city, risk and reward, the fat pump of thick blood up the slim neck, the stirring strength of hands.

Chloe's flapping her flappy legs and slap-clapping her clappy palms because she knows that past the room with the red floor and glass doors where it's cooler and there's no sun the room with the buttons rides up and after the ride up the narrow room not where the cute strange doggies with their black gums and such teeth sniff and sniff and lick or sudden loudest ripping vanishes or strangers stare and say so many words like the flowers and the leafy trees but at the end of the narrow room is the door where daddy needs his keys and that's Chloe's home and Chloe's home is where mommy and daddy and everything is and everything is in its place and everything is in its thing.

Click and Kiss

"Um-ma!" Her daughter and the father of her daughter surprise Viv as she's sloppying into the kitchen: Clive, removing his sunglasses, sweaty, sexy; Chloe in her blue hat, open-eyed laugh and arms reaching as fun as the whole Spring weekend. What a snatch of the dead uninterruption will do.

"You're back," Viv declares.

"We went to the market. We bought fish. We met some dogs."

"All that?"

"All that."

Their casual kiss is mélange of market scruffiness, fresh air, sleepy raggedness, unexpected rush. Chloe's stroller strap clicks open and she springs into her mother's swoop.

His and Hers

All this belongs to her, the healthy man fidgeting the grocery bags from the back of the stroller, the piquant ladybug standing—a new skill—and holding an edge of the coffee table, starting to pick plastic animal figurines out of a mixing bowl. They are hers and she is theirs.

He has to put all the market stuff away. He has to tug the plastic bags from the stroller's undercarriage. Fish goes in the fridge. Kale? Kale goes in the fridge. He forgot apples. Tarragon goes in the fridge. Spinach goes in the fridge. Tomatoes for some reason go on the countertop. With his elbow he budges open the fridge door. The sight of beer on the top shelf sends the small future of a happy afternoon in the park through his shoulder nerves like massage.

One and Many

Chloe's goes to the coffee table to sort the plastic animal figurines into their proper places under her mother's approval. The walrus goes beside the polar bear. The dappled cow goes beside the walrus. Beside the polar bear goes the brontosaurus. The coyote goes beside the dappled cow. The moose goes beside the coyote.

"Sleep any?" Clive asks. She seems calm so he's calm.

"I even dreamt. About Tim."

"What did you dream about Tim?"

"I can't remember much. He mentioned W.H. Auden, I think."

Clive assumes Viv slept with Tim in her dream but the interloper has no right to jealousy—Tim's the sword between them in their bed and the shibboleth on their joining tongues. Chloe decides that all animals are one and grabs walrus, bear, dappled cow, brontosaurus, coyote, moose, camel, bison up together in both hands and dumps the mangled plastic tangle back in the mixing bowl.

Living and Dead

Separately, suddenly, Clive and Viv remember the linguistic fact that we don't possess the dead, we are possessed by the dead. Grammar don't lie.

"Did he ask about me?" Clive asks.

"Selfish bastard."

"I know, I know, but I was just thinking about him on the way to the market, about how happy we all were together. I mean, given adultery, insanity."

"So said the living man about his dead friend."

"Maybe."

Do they possess us like pets? Do they run us like cars needing maintenance and gas? Or do they hire us like cabs just for a ride around a town with no particular destination in mind?

Sudden Desire

Chloe wants Chloe realizes
Chloe wants Chloe remem-
bers What does Chloe
want? Chloe wants? Chloe
waaaants wants Chloe
wants wants wants
HOME STUFF FOOD
MOM SOFT LOVE

Mom and Dad

Yeah honey? You hungry? Well aren't we all? And we'll just wait for the pillow to come. No, no, no, not yet sweetie, because mommy's arm will fall off. But it's breakfast! Breakfast soon. Daddy's just run into your bedroom for the pillow and then we won't even have to go into the dark. Isn't that nice? Isn't that fun? We'll just stay right here in the light.

Clive strides around them, around the other side of Viv who is lifting Chloe into her arms, and strides down the hall to the baby's room.

Clive is looking for something. Clive is looking for love. Secure love in one time and one place. But he is looking for something else too. The breastfeeding pillow tucked behind the rocking chair.

Mother and Child

The pillow has soaked up so many spilled drops of tenderness that the smell alone is peace to the ladybug. Clive watches Viv, stacking their daughter on its softness, shielding Chloe's face from the outside light, the resurgent noisesomeness of the street below. He watches Chloe's frail and expectant face latching to the offered breast squeezed, sucking the nipple tingle for all the world and its fullness. From the window, a growing smell of newness breaks over their little family, and this time there's no confusing it with fall; the mess of spring brings with it the delicacy of hope, which is not frail, ravaging the blood-warm skin-cool air. Without anybody thinking, the gift of the world in all its fullness spurts, the strength of life in all seasons begins again.

ABOUT THE AUTHOR

Stephen Marche is a novelist, columnist and enemy of boredom.
His books include *Raymond and Hannah*, *Shining at the Bottom
of the Sea* and *How Shakespeare Changed Everything*. He lives
in Toronto with his wife and two children.

THIS BOOK WAS DESIGNED AND SET INTO TYPE BY ANDREW STEEVES WITH MUCH CONSULTATION AND DIRECTION FROM STEPHEN MARCHE ❦ THE ILLUSTRATION OF THE NEW YORK CITY SUBWAY MAP WAS CREATED BY JACK MCMASTER & ANDREW STEEVES

THE
BODY OF THIS
BOOK WAS TYPESET IN

HURONIA

a robust neohumanist type
designed by W. Ross Mills

TYPES IN SUPPORTING ROLES INCLUDE
Gill Sans & Classic Grotesque (MONO-
TYPE) 𝕎illiam Morris's Troy (P22)
Ambassador Script (CANADA
TYPE) *and a fleuron from*
Rialto (*df* TYPE) ❦

Text copyright © Stephen Marche, 2012

All rights reserved. No part of this publication may be reproduced in any form without the prior written consent of the publisher. Any requests for the photocopying of any part of this book should be directed in writing to Access Copyright: The Canadian Copyright Licensing Agency. Gaspereau Press acknowledges the support of the Canada Council for the Arts and the Nova Scotia Department of Communities, Culture & Heritage.

Typeset by Andrew Steeves & printed offset and bound under the direction of Gary Dunfield at Gaspereau Press, Kentville, Nova Scotia.

7   6   5   4   3   2

Library and Archives Canada Cataloguing in Publication

Marche, Stephen
Love and the mess we're in / Stephen Marche.

ISBN 978-1-55447-107-2

I. Title.

PS8626.A723L69 2012   C813'.6   C2012-905455-0

GASPEREAU PRESS LIMITED ¶ GARY DUNFIELD
& ANDREW STEEVES ¶ PRINTERS & PUBLISHERS
47 Church Avenue, Kentville, Nova Scotia, B4N 2M7
www.gaspereau.com